And for just a minute, he allowed himself to wonder—if things had gone differently, would he and Trish have had a son? With red hair and big blue eyes?

Trish had wanted a child. Once she'd finally made the decision to get married, she'd jumped in with both feet.

When he'd had to leave, had been forced to disappear, he sweated out the first couple months, until he was sure that he hadn't left her pregnant. He still wouldn't have been able to go back, but he'd have figured out some way to ensure that his child was well taken care of. Just like he'd figured out ways to ensure that Trish was safe, protected.

He'd done a good job.

But now something had gone wrong and Trish was paying the price.

DEEP SECRETS

BEVERLY LONG

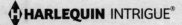

For Kathy and Randy and their family, who have made us feel very welcome in Missouri.

Recycling programs
for this product may
not exist in your area.

ISBN-13: 978-0-373-69911-7

Deep Secrets

Copyright © 2016 by Beverly R. Long

Printed in U.S.A.

Beverly Long enjoys the opportunity to write her own stories. She has both a bachelor's and a master's degree in business and more than twenty years of experience as a human resources director. She considers her books to be a great success if they compel the reader to stay up way past their bedtime. Beverly loves to hear from readers. Visit beverlylong.com, or like her at Facebook.com/beverlylong.romance.

Books by Beverly Long

Return to Ravesville

Hidden Witness
Agent Bride
Urgent Pursuit
Deep Secrets

The Men from Crow Hollow

Hunted
Stalked
Trapped

The Detectives

Deadly Force
Secure Location

Visit the Author Profile page at
Harlequin.com for more titles.

CAST OF CHARACTERS

Trish Wright-Roper—Widowed four years earlier, she's determined to finally move on. But then her trusted friend is murdered and she's kidnapped. The impossible only gets worse when the only man who can save her is her husband...who apparently isn't dead after all.

Rafe Roper—Four years ago, when his past caught up with him, he took extreme measures to ensure Trish's safety. Now her kidnappers have sent proof: she'll die soon. He's got one last chance to save her, but it means that she'll hate him forever.

Bernie Wilberts—He rents a cottage to Trish, and she's thankful for the last-minute reservation. But does he have an ulterior motive for offering such a good deal?

Barry North—Trish met him online and when he proposes that they meet in person, she agrees. But is he really just interested in dinner?

Mary Ann Fikus—She's been a longtime customer of the Wright Here, Wright Now Café. Why now is she suddenly so intent upon sharing a good deal on a cottage rental?

Big Tony and Anthony Paradini—Father and son, they abduct Trish but insinuate that she's a means to an end. Somebody else is giving the orders, but who could that be?

Luciano Maladucci—Rafe believes he's a terrorist. Is he also behind Trish's kidnapping?

Demi Maladucci—For years, he's disassociated himself from the rest of the family. When Rafe sees that changing, he can't help but wonder what it might mean.

Kevin Leonard—Rafe has trusted and respected him for years, but when he realizes that the man has purposefully gotten close to Trish, Rafe suspects that he is very dangerous.

Chapter One

Trish Wright-Roper stuck the fork tines through the paper napkin, ruining it. Normally, she didn't mind rolling silverware. It was a mindless activity, really. But on a day like today, when her brain was too busy remembering, it was irritating her beyond reason.

She could hear Milo finishing up in the kitchen. Earlier he'd dropped a steam table pan onto the tile floor and the clang had echoed through the empty café. She'd gone back to investigate and he'd been staring at the pan, his face flushed with anger.

Not at himself. Not at the pan. Not even at her.

For her. Because everyone who knew Trish well knew that four years ago today, Rafe Roper had died and her heart had been broken. And everybody who cared about her, which definitely included Milo, was on edge. No one would admit it, though. Instead, they'd practically turn somersaults to get her to think of something else.

Milo was no different. "What do you say you and me catch a movie in Hamerton tonight?" he asked, coming out of the kitchen. The man's hair was pulled back from his face in a tight ponytail and it hung practically to the middle of his back. He was an ex-con who'd applied for work just weeks after Rafe's death. He'd been a lifesaver because she'd been in no shape to work, to hold up her share of the responsibilities.

"You hate movies," she said. "You think it's ridiculous to pay ten dollars to see something that you'll be able to see for nothing in just a couple of months."

"Yeah, but there's this one I've really been wanting to watch."

She shook her head. "No, there isn't. You know that Summer and I usually watch some silly romantic comedy today and you also know that she's not due back from her honeymoon until tomorrow. You're *filling in*."

He drummed his thumb on the counter, a sure sign that he was frustrated. "She hated that she was going to be gone. I promised her that I had this."

When her twin sister, Summer, had married handsome Bray Hollister, the love of her life, several months earlier, they'd postponed their honeymoon until Summer's kids could take a week off school. Bray had made the honeymoon arrangements and Summer hadn't had the heart to tell him that she wanted to be back in Ravesville a day earlier.

But her twin had felt terrible about it. She and Trish had discussed it. Trish had assured her it was fine. Summer had wisely not mentioned that she intended to draft her own replacement.

"Come on. Your sister is going to be mad at me if I don't get this right," Milo said, proving that he was willing to play upon every emotion.

"Are you scared of her or her tough-guy husband?"

"Both."

She smiled at him. Milo wasn't afraid of anything. Over the years he'd been at the café, they'd had more than one disruptive customer. It was bound to happen, especially in a café that attracted one-timers, the people driving through on their way somewhere else. In those instances, with a minimum of fuss and mess, Milo would have his arm around the customer, gently pushing him out of the café, with a stern warning not to bother to come back.

He was prepared to defend them. One time when he'd been lying on the kitchen floor, fixing a temperamental fryer, she'd spied an ankle holster. She knew as an ex-con he likely wasn't supposed to have a gun. She also believed that he carried it purely for protection. For himself. For her and Summer. When he realized that she'd seen the gun, he challenged her. "You have a problem with this?" he said.

She didn't really like guns. When she'd been married to Rafe, he'd owned one and had insisted that she learn to shoot it. Had said that he wanted her to learn for safety reasons, that if there was a gun in the house, every adult needed to know how to use it safely. She'd gone along with his wishes and had got good enough that she was confident that she wouldn't shoot her own foot off. So when Milo asked, she'd shaken her head. "No problem here."

He'd smiled and gone back to fixing the fryer. As she walked past, he muttered, "Always did think she was a smart girl."

Now she stared at the man who'd become much more friend than employee. "Don't worry about me. I'll be fine."

He studied her. Kept drumming his thumb. The poor digit was going to be bruised. "I suspect Rafe would want you to keep living," he said finally.

"How do you know? You never met him," she challenged, her words clipped. She could usually count on

Milo not to offer advice. It was always a rare reprieve and it made her mad that even that had changed.

"I…I just think he would. People have to go on. Even when it's hard."

He probably knew something about that. After all, he'd survived prison. "I know you mean well," she said, her tone kinder than before. "I've actually taken that advice," she added hesitantly.

"How so?"

"I signed up for an online dating site," she said.

Thumb stopped, head jerked up. "You never said anything about that."

She hadn't. To anyone, not even Summer.

"Any matches?" he asked.

"One that looks interesting," she admitted. "We've been emailing back and forth for a couple of weeks."

"You need to be careful with sites like that," Milo said, his voice heavy with concern. "Why don't you give me this guy's name? I'll check him out for you."

She could do that or she could call Chase Hollister, Bray's brother, who'd taken over the role of Ravesville chief of police recently, and ask him to run a check. "I haven't said that I'll meet him yet," she said. "If I do that, I'll decide then whether he needs to submit his fingerprints. In triplicate, of course. Maybe give a blood sample."

He smiled, as much as Milo ever did. "I realize you're not the foolish type, Trish. But I care about you. A lot of people do."

"I know. And believe me, it helps. Now, let's finish up here. I want to go home. It's been good to have Raney and Nalana Hollister here to help in Summer's absence, but it's still been extra work. I just want to go home and take a hot shower and crawl into bed."

"You're still planning to take a few days off next week."

"I am. Payback."

"Summer will be delighted. You never take time off."

She rarely did. And on the occasional day that she did play hooky, she generally worked in her yard, which had a never-ending supply of projects. Weeds to pull. Plants to move. Trees to trim.

But this time, she was doing none of that. She felt a little guilty about not confiding in Milo, but he worried way too much about her and Summer.

"Maybe we could go fishing one day," he said. "I could teach you a few things."

She held up a hand. "I do not want to hear one more time about that bass you caught."

He tossed his head and laughed. "It's not bragging when a man has pictures."

"I suppose not. I'll let you know if I'm available to be humiliated," she added, picking up a fork.

He looked at her pile of silverware. "I've got one more load of dishes and then the garbage. Will you be ready in ten minutes?"

When it was just the two of them at the end of the night, he always insisted that they leave together. "You bet," she said and watched him walk back to the kitchen.

She glanced out the front windows of the Wright Here, Wright Now Café. All the parking spaces in front of the café were empty. The town got quiet fast, even on a pretty spring evening. Tulips had bloomed last week in the flower box in front of the law office across the street, and now they were dancing in the light wind.

Didn't matter how unbearable the winter was, those flowers always came back. And she had, too. Yes, she'd suffered a great loss. But she had much to be thankful for. A wonderful sister. Her nephew, Keagan, and her sweet little niece, Adie. Her new brother-in-law, who made sure she knew that every one of the Hollisters considered her family.

And now that she was almost thirty-eight years old, it was time to get on with her life.

A soft sob escaped and she looked around the empty café, grateful that no one was there to witness her lapse. Most of the time she was able to fool people. She could laugh and joke with the best of them. Only a precious few knew how much she mourned Rafe, who'd had the bad luck to go on a stupid float trip with his buddies. Only a precious few knew that sometimes she would go to the river and stare at the murky depths, so angry that it had taken her husband from her, not even generous enough to give her back a body to bury.

She rolled the last knife, fork and spoon and gently laid the napkin on the top of the stack. Then she carefully slid the tray of rolled silverware under the counter, where it would be easy to grab in the morning. Tables would fill up fast. She loved it when the place was really busy, when there were customers to wait on, tables to clear and money to take at the cash register. She loved the noise and the energy of people enjoying a good meal.

And while the café had a very different feel at the end of the day, when it was empty and quiet, it was satisfying to sit on a counter stool and look around at the clean floor, the shiny counters, the freshly washed pie case and know that she and Summer had built this from practically nothing.

They had purchased the café more than five years earlier. The previous owners had let the place get run-down and business had dwindled. Once she and Summer had signed on the dotted line, they'd had to close the place for a month just to get it ready to open again. Walls had been painted, floors and counters replaced, booths and tables repaired and all new dishes acquired. Then they'd tackled the kitchen. A new grill had been installed, the walk-in refrigerator scrubbed from top to bottom, and best of all, they'd purchased a new dishwasher.

Summer wanted the day shift to be home with her kids at night. That had been just fine with Trish. She'd always been a bit of a night owl. They'd hired a small staff and opened their doors to the grateful appreciation of all the other business owners on Main Street. The small downtown had been in danger of going the way that most small towns had, with empty storefronts and dilapidated buildings. There were high hopes for the Wright Here, Wright Now Café.

Summer and Trish Wright had grown up in Ravesville and people were willing to give the place a try. Word spread quickly that the service and food were top-notch and business had grown rapidly.

Four months after they'd opened, Trish had been just about to lock the doors the night that Rafe had blown into town. Literally. It had been a hot summer day and the weather forecasters had droned on about the possibility of tornadoes. At nine o'clock, like every night, she'd hung the Closed sign in the window. Had been grateful that the restaurant had cleared out by eight thirty. She had already sent Daisy, her night cook, home, because the woman was deathly afraid of storms.

She'd been walking back to the kitchen, to do one final sweep of the space, when pounding on the front door got her attention. She'd turned, locked eyes with the handsome stranger and, as crazy as it seemed, realized immediately that her life was about to experience a fundamental shift.

She'd unlocked the door just as the Ravesville tornado sirens started ringing. The stranger had smiled at her. "I think it's about to get interesting," he'd said.

She'd had no idea.

The café didn't have a basement, so she and the man had ridden out the storm sitting on the floor in the small space between the back wall and the counter, protected from the possibility of flying glass. They'd each had two pieces of banana cream pie because he'd convinced her if they were both about to die, there was no sense worrying about calories.

The café had survived the storm, and when he'd said goodbye, he'd touched her cheek. She'd thought she'd seen the last of her mysterious stranger, that he'd been a one-timer, but then two nights later, he was back, asking her to dinner. By the following weekend, they'd been lovers.

Neither one of them were kids. She'd been thirty-three and he was just a year older. She hadn't been especially interested in marriage. She was well aware of how miserable Summer was with her husband, Gary Blake, and she didn't have any interest in making a similar mistake. When Rafe asked her to move in with him after six weeks of dating, she said no. She liked her independence and didn't see a need to give it up.

But Rafe Roper knew how to wear a girl down. He was an amazing lover but it was more than that. He was different than the other men that she'd dated. Most important, he made her laugh. Every day. And he remembered all the little things. She'd get up in the morning and there would be chocolate doughnuts on her front porch. He'd have dropped them by early on his way to Hamerton, where he was part of the construction crew building the new mall. He would send her flowers. Never roses, because she'd mentioned just once that they weren't her favorites. He sent lilies. Always lilies.

He was a fabulous cook and could make all her favorites, including eggplant parmigiana and shrimp scampi. He'd teased her mercilessly about owning a café and being barely capable of boiling water.

She and Summer still had work to do on the café and he was always willing to lend a hand, to fix a door or paint a wall. She could still see Summer standing near the pie case, telling Trish that she'd be a fool to let him get away.

And Trish knew she was right. So when Rafe asked her to marry him after they'd been dating for three months, she didn't hesitate to say yes. And he didn't give her time to think about her decision. They were married just two weeks later. Then they bought a house together, too big for just the two of them, but she'd started dreaming about babies to fill the empty rooms. Babies with dark eyes and an amazing smile, just like their daddy.

And life was pretty darn near perfect.

Nine months later, he was dead. He'd gone back east to visit a friend who was sick. She'd assumed it was a dear friend because when he'd returned, she'd sensed that he was still upset. When he'd left the next day on a float trip with his buddies on the construction crew, she'd hoped it would cheer him up.

His raft had overturned and his body had never been recovered.

Then it was not just the rooms of her house that were empty.

Her heart. Her soul.

Her spirit.

She'd wished she was dead, too. But she'd lived. And somehow, someway, had managed to crawl her way back. Didn't expect to ever feel full again but had developed an odd contentment with the emptiness. Except for nights like this, when it became unbearable.

She'd expected to feel blue today. That was probably why earlier in the week she'd jumped at something Mary Ann Fikus had said. M.A., as everyone called her, worked at the bank and ate lunch almost every day at the café. She was just back from a week in the Ozarks. She'd been going on about the cottage where she'd stayed.

Trish had been to the Ozarks, the lake-filled, mountainous area in southwest Missouri, several times and had even stayed at the particular lake that M.A. had visited. It was a lovely area.

And when M.A. described the cottage, it had sounded like the perfect place to rest and read books and maybe, just maybe, fish. Thinking there was little chance it would be available at such late notice, Trish had called the owner and been pleasantly surprised that it was. She'd assumed they would want a credit card to hold it, but Bernie Wilberts had told her that she could simply leave a check on the table when she left. She'd been very careful to explain that she would arrive on Sunday, but he'd told her it didn't matter, that the cottage was empty. He'd given her the combination code for the lock on the door.

If Summer had been around, Trish would have told her about her plans. She'd thought about telling Milo, but given his propensity to worry about her, she'd thought better of it. She'd tell him just before she left town.

She turned to walk back to the kitchen and stopped abruptly when there was intense pounding on the door. Her heart leaped in her chest. It was like that night so long ago. She turned.

And through the glass, she saw Keagan, her fourteen-year-old nephew. With five-year-old Adie next to him. Summer and Bray were a little slower to get out of the SUV.

She opened the door and the four of them tumbled in. "What are you doing home?" she asked, hugging each of the kids. Then Bray. Finally, her sister. She hung on an extra minute. She knew why her sister was here. "You shouldn't have," she whispered.

Summer shook her head. "When I told Bray what today was," she said, grabbing her new husband's hand, "he changed our flight so that we could get back. He insisted."

She rolled her eyes in her brother-in-law's direction. "I guess I do understand why she loves you," she said.

Bray winked at her and focused on Adie, who had found her favorite seat at the counter and was whirling on the stool at warp speed.

"How are you feeling?" Trish asked, looking at Summer's still-flat stomach.

"Fine. But anything that went in circles at Disney World was Bray's domain. I stood on the sidelines and ate orange Popsicles."

It was unbelievable that Summer and Bray would be

adding to their family in just seven more months. More proof that life really did go on. She drew in a breath and smiled. "Well, Milo was insisting on a movie tonight. I guess you're all excited to see *Pretty Woman* one more time."

"How did you know that was my favorite movie?" Bray asked with a straight face.

Summer lightly punched her husband's biceps before turning back to Trish. "I'm sure you're glad that you're not holding down the fort alone any longer. Next week, I want you to rest up. You will take a couple of days off, right?"

"I think I will," Trish said.

"Where's Milo?" Summer asked, moving quickly to the next topic.

She could tell them both about her plans. "Taking out the garbage. I'll get him."

Trish went through the swinging door that connected the dining room to the kitchen. No Milo. The back door was open just a fraction of an inch, letting the cool spring air blow in. The light near the back door was on.

"Milo," she called, walking toward the door. "Summer and Bray are—"

She opened the back door and almost tripped. On a body.

Milo. *Oh my God.* "What happened?" she asked, dropping to her knees.

There was blood everywhere. On his body, on the pavement, running out of the side of his mouth. "Milo," she cried, reaching to lift his head off the cold, hard ground.

"Trish," he said, his breaths raspy. "Tell Rafe they know."

He closed his eyes and she started to scream.

Chapter Two

Tell Rafe they know.

Trish sat on the edge of a booth, her feet flat on the floor, her eyes closed. Hoping that the world would stop spinning. Somebody had draped a blanket over her.

Maybe it had been Summer. Or Bray. Or maybe even Chase Hollister, who hadn't even been on the job for six months. He was about to investigate his first murder.

Milo was dead. Knifed to death. Gutted like a fish. That was what she'd heard one of the volunteers from the fire and rescue squad say before Bray had grabbed his shirt collar and jerked him out of the room. The man had come back, said a quiet apology in her direction and been more respectful until Chase finally let them take Milo's body from the scene. Of course, it had seemed like hours before they'd moved him off the cold ground. At some point, more police had arrived. They were still here. Portable lighting had been set up behind the café, making it look even more surreal.

The images in her head were disjointed. Opening the door, practically stumbling over the body. Blood. So much blood. Bray whipping the door open, pulling her back.

Thank goodness for Bray. He'd taken charge. She and Summer had been hustled back inside the café, where Keagan and Adie waited, scared to death that their aunt had been screaming. He must have called the police, too, because within minutes Chase Hollister had arrived, looking very serious.

At some point, Cal Hollister and his pretty wife, Nalana, had arrived and taken Summer and the kids away from all the ugliness. Her twin hadn't wanted to leave, but she'd already thrown up three times and Bray had had enough. "I'll call you tomorrow," Summer said, as Nalana was guiding her out of the door. "We need to talk about a funeral."

Milo didn't have family. It would be up to them. He wouldn't want a funeral. And if he'd known about her trip, then he'd have been mad as hell at her if she canceled so that they could have one.

But funerals weren't for the dead. They were for the living, to make it easier to say goodbye. They would definitely have a funeral.

THEN SHE HAD watched Summer and the kids leave. She wasn't worried about them. Bray's youngest brother, Cal, had been a Navy SEAL. Nalana, his new bride, was still an FBI agent.

She'd stared at the floor after that. Until she'd finally got so tired that she needed to close her eyes.

"Trish," she heard someone say.

She wanted to ignore it, to pretend that the past several hours hadn't happened. But that wasn't an option.

She lifted her head. Chase was squatting down in front of her, his eyes full of concern.

"How are you doing?" he asked.

She licked her dry lips. "He was a good man," she said, choosing to ignore the question. She wasn't up to pretending that she was fine. She was so damn tired of always pretending that she was fine.

"Yes, he was," Chase said. "And we will find the person who did this. I promise you."

If anyone could, it was probably Chase. He'd been a cop in St. Louis before coming back to Ravesville, ostensibly to get his deceased parents' house ready for sale but really to guard a key witness in a murder case. He'd done more than just guard the witness. He'd married her. And now Raney Hollister was one of Trish's favorite people.

"Was there anyone unusual in the café tonight or maybe even within the last couple of days?"

The question wasn't unexpected. She'd been trying to think of the same thing for the past hour. "I don't think so," she said. "We had a few strangers, of course." That wasn't unusual. Travelers. Usually vacationers. People in need of a hot meal and a cup of coffee. "But nobody that I considered unusual or suspicious."

"Did Milo have any visitors or receive any unusual telephone calls that you're aware of?"

"No. I don't think he had any plans for after work because he'd asked me if I wanted to see a movie."

She saw Chase exchange a quick glance with Bray. "Did you often watch movies together?" Chase asked, probably wondering if he'd missed a romantic connection between her and Milo.

"Never," she said. "But he knew that today was a tough day for me."

Another glance between Chase and Bray. Oh, for goodness' sake, Bray didn't have to explain this. She was a big girl. "My husband, Rafe Roper, died four years ago today," she said.

"I'm sorry," Chase said.

She believed him. Chase Hollister was a good man. She'd known him since he was a kid. Which was why she was going to tell him everything, even though her mind hadn't made sense of it yet.

"Milo said something before he died."

Bray's head whipped up. This was news to him.

"What was that?" Chase said gently.

"'Tell Rafe they know.'"

Chase didn't look at Bray this time. He was staring intently at her. "You're sure that's what he said?"

"Yes."

Chase stood up, walked over to the window, looked out at the street. Finally, he turned. "Did Milo know your husband?"

"No. Rafe was already dead before he came to work here."

"Did the two of you frequently talk about Rafe?"

"No. I don't discuss Rafe with many people. But Milo and I had been talking earlier in the evening and his name came up."

"Is it possible that Milo was confused? That your conversation earlier in the evening was on his mind, and that's why he mentioned him before he died?"

"I guess," she said, her tone flat. It made as much sense as anything. But she'd never seen Milo confused or discombobulated about anything. He was always calm, always controlled. But then again, she'd never seen him bleeding to death on the dirty pavement, either.

"I don't know," she said, her voice breaking. "I just don't know and it's driving me crazy."

Chase reached out for her hand. It probably wasn't police protocol, but given that his brother was married to her twin sister, she and Chase were family. "It's going to be okay," he said. "I know hearing something like that would be very upsetting. But he was dying. Losing lots of blood quickly. He wouldn't have been thinking clearly."

She'd been telling herself the same thing. But for some strange reason, it really irritated her to hear someone else say it. "They were his last words. I think they were important to him," she snapped.

"Of course," Chase said.

Bray stood up. "I think I should take Trish back to my house," he said.

When Summer and Bray had got married, Bray had moved into the small house that Summer had rented with her two children. They were building a new home but the walls had just gone up. "You don't have extra space," she said. "I'll go to my own house."

"You can stay with Raney and me," Chase said immediately.

She did not want to stay with anyone. She was strung so tight that she was about to lose it. "Is there any reason to think that I'm in danger, that the attack on Milo had something to do with me or Summer or the café?"

"We have no way of knowing that," Chase said. "Milo was attacked from behind. As best as I can tell, he was in the process of putting the garbage into the Dumpster when he was stabbed. Based on what Bray has told me, I understand you opened the door to check on him and he was already on the ground. Whoever had done this was gone."

She nodded. "He'd been in prison. Do you think it could be someone from his past, someone who maybe held a grudge?" She was grasping at straws but she so desperately wanted to make sense of it.

"I don't know," Chase said. "I've asked for help from

the state. They have more sophisticated resources than we have to process the scene. We're going to be done here in just a little while, but I'd prefer it if you could keep the café closed tomorrow, just in case."

Saturdays were usually busy days. "I'll put a sign on the door," she said, getting up to find paper and a pen. The sign probably wasn't necessary. It was a sure bet that at least one of the volunteer fire and rescue squad would tell his or her spouse what had happened here tonight and it would spread like wildfire. By morning, everyone in the small town would know why the café wasn't open.

It was one of the reasons she hadn't said anything before this about Milo's last words. She hadn't wanted it to be overheard.

Because if one well-meaning person asked her what she thought about it, she might explode. She didn't know what she thought. *Tell Rafe* implied something that she couldn't even fathom. *They know.* Know what, for God's sake? "I want to go home," she said. "To my house. I have Duke. He won't let anyone get near me." It was true. The German shepherd was fiercely protective, had been since the day he'd wandered up to her doorstep without any tags. She'd searched for an owner for a week, even putting an ad in the paper, but no one had come forward. Duke had become her dog.

"A dog isn't much protection against a bullet," Chase said gently.

"This was a knife, not a bullet."

"You don't know that's the only available weapon," he said.

"The café emptied out at least a half hour before we closed. I was alone in the dining room, clearly visible if someone outside had bothered to look in the window. If they wanted to harm me, they had a chance. But they waited until Milo took the trash out. I think this was about Milo, not about me."

"Even with that final comment?" Bray asked.

"Like Chase said, Milo was dying. He might have been confused." She picked up her purse and kissed her brother-in-law on the cheek. "Thank you," she said. "Thank you for bringing Summer home early, thank you for being here and for having the wherewithal to respond."

Then she turned to Chase. "I trust you, Chase. With every bone in my body. I know that you'll do everything you can to find Milo's killer. He was a wonderful friend and he didn't deserve to die like this." Then she leaned in and gave him a quick hug.

Bray picked up his keys from the counter. "At least let me follow you home and make sure you get inside safely."

The Hollister men were very protective of the women they loved, and by virtue of being Summer's sister, she was automatically included in their circle. "Fine. Let's go."

HER FOUR-BEDROOM RANCH house was too big for one person, and tonight, more than ever, she felt as if she was drifting from room to room, looking for ghosts. She was grateful, though, for the silence.

Bray had been true to his word. He'd left, a worried look on his face, after he'd checked every room and the garage. She'd assured him that she'd set the alarm immediately and she had.

Now she stood in her kitchen and Duke crowded in next to her, almost as if he knew that something wasn't quite right. He was poking his nose at her knees, and when she reached down to pet him, she realized that there was blood on her dark blue pants.

Milo's blood. She hadn't seen it before, but when she'd knelt next to the body, the blood had got on her.

"Oh, Milo," she sobbed, catching hold of the kitchen counter to keep herself upright. *Tell Rafe they know.* "What did you mean?"

With jerky movements, she peeled off every stitch of her clothes. Then naked, she stuffed them into the kitchen garbage can. She roughly yanked out the plastic bag insert and tied it up tight. With heavy arms, she tossed the bag by the door that led to her garage.

Then, feeling very old and weary, she walked back to her bedroom and straight into the adjoining bath. She turned on the shower, as hot as she could stand it. And when she stepped under the spray, she let the tears that she'd held back all night run down her face.

Her chest heaved with her sobs and she braced herself against the wall.

She wasn't stupid. *Tell Rafe.* That implied that Rafe was alive. Was that even possible? His body had never been found. But what would keep him away? What would keep a husband away from his wife?

Four years. Four long years.

Over fourteen hundred days of heartache.

It just wasn't possible. Rafe would never hurt her like that.

RAFE HOPED THERE were no snakes in the damn grass. It was damp and scratchy and smelled like a herd of cattle had passed through. He'd arrived before dawn and had been on his stomach for the past several hours. He badly wanted a cup of hot coffee. But he didn't move.

Windows were open in the villa and music drifted up the hill. When the song changed, his gut tightened up.

They played that one at his wedding. And in the morning, his beautiful bride had been humming it.

She'd been so happy. And he'd thought it would last until balls started dropping out of the air. Accidents, some said. He knew better.

His trusted coworkers had been murdered. He didn't care what anybody said.

And he suspected the man inside, who was probably about to sit down to breakfast with his family, was responsible. Luciano Maladucci. Richer than several European countries put together and more evil than most could even imagine, he delighted in playing chess with people's lives.

Unfortunately, Rafe hadn't been able to prove Maladucci was behind the deaths. It had been his sole focus his first six months back, but every lead turned into a dead end. He had to stop when his boss told him in no uncertain terms to *let it go.*

He let it go. At least as far as most people knew. But he'd found another way to tighten the noose around this man's neck. One way or the other, he was going to see him behind prison bars.

With his binoculars picking up every detail, he watched a Ferrari Spider turn into the circle drive. What was the youngest Maladucci son doing here? The older son and his family lived in the east wing of the villa. It was rare for the two brothers to be together, probably because the younger brother had slept with the older brother's wife three years ago.

Real friendly, the Maladuccis.

Real deadly, too.

He felt the buzz from his cell phone. His private cell

phone. What the hell? Milo wasn't supposed to check in until Sunday. It was Saturday.

He shifted, pulled his phone out and realized it wasn't Milo, but someone else he trusted explicitly. He stared at the text message.

Milo is dead.

There were a hundred possibilities. Like a heart attack or a stroke?

But none of those would have warranted a special message. No. This message meant that there was danger. And it was headed toward Trish.

Chapter Three

She stayed in the shower until the hot water ran out. When she got out, she considered not drying her waist-length hair but knew that it would be a tangled mess in the morning if she went to bed with it wet.

She should have cut it years ago. But when she'd been married to Rafe, he'd convinced her to keep it long. *I love your hair*, he used to say. *Your beautiful red hair. The night of the storm, I saw it through the window of the café. It looked like liquid fire. I thought I'd never seen anything quite so wonderful.*

After he'd died, she couldn't bear to do any more than trim the ends. Wore it pulled back most of the time in a low ponytail.

Tell Rafe they know.

She sat down hard on the edge of the bathtub. It was crazy but she was so angry at Milo. The poor man was dead and she was furious that he'd said something like that and then died.

She was a bad person. Horrible. A man was dead and all she could think about was herself.

She jabbed the on button and held the dryer for too long in one spot, burning her scalp. Ten minutes later, she gave up. Her hair was still damp but she was so damn tired. She picked up her toothbrush, spread some tooth-paste and halfheartedly brushed. When she tossed her toothbrush back onto the counter, a memory hit her so hard that she almost doubled over.

Rafe putting his toothbrush back just so, in exactly the same spot every time. His shaving cream and razor, too. *Everything in its place*, he used to say, lightheartedly poking fun at himself. Before she'd married him, she'd considered herself pretty neat and organized. But Rafe had been the king of patterns and order. She'd noticed it slowly, over time. He kept very little paper around, usually just a small pile of unpaid bills. If you asked, he could tell you, in the order it appeared, what was on his desk at any one time.

He never made a big deal out of it. And she had never taken it too seriously until one night they'd come home from a movie in Hamerton, entered the house, and he'd sensed that something was different. He'd grabbed her, pulled her behind him, and the gun that he always carried on him had been in his hand. *The hallway light wasn't on when we left*, he had whispered in her ear.

He'd inspected the whole house but had come up empty. But she could tell that he was bothered by the incident. It wasn't until she finally checked her cell phone, which she'd turned off at the movies, that she heard the message from Summer. She'd stopped over to borrow a dress.

When she'd told Rafe, he'd waved it off. She could tell he didn't want to discuss it. But she hadn't forgotten it. She had seen a side of her husband that night that was fascinating. It was not as if he'd morphed into someone new. No, it was more subtle than that.

He was still Rafe, the handsome construction worker who had stolen her heart and made her laugh every day.

But he was someone else, too. Someone very capable. Someone fearless.

Someone, she suspected, who would do whatever it took to protect her and their home. He'd handled the gun expertly. She'd been in awe, really.

And she'd started paying more attention to the things around her. Noticing when things changed. It was like playing a game where there was no score and she was competing only against herself. She got better at it every day. Nobody got new glasses, highlighted their hair or had their teeth fixed that she didn't pick up on it. It was just crazy small stuff but she had fun with it.

It was only one of the many ways that loving Rafe had changed her.

She left the bathroom. She didn't bother to dress. Simply crawled into bed naked. She could hear Duke pacing in front of her door, his nails scratching against the wood floor. "Good night, Duke," she said, knowing that he wouldn't settle down if that nighttime ritual wasn't observed.

The pacing quieted and she knew the big dog had taken his spot outside her door. He'd knock his hind end on the door at five the next morning, ready to go out. Until then, she could sleep.

Except that every time she closed her eyes, she could see poor Milo. After a half hour, she gave up and turned on her light. Duke immediately whined, letting her know that he knew that something wasn't right. She opened the bedroom door. "We're leaving early," she said.

She had to. She absolutely had to leave this house that she had bought with Rafe, where she had made plans, dreamed big. The memories of Rafe were still too strong here. She could see him at the stove, wearing his jeans low on his hips and no shirt, waving a spatula in her direction. Could see him snoozing on the couch, a book open on his chest. Could see him walk across the kitchen naked for that first cup of coffee in the morning.

Could practically smell his earthy masculine scent.

Was it because it was the anniversary of his death? Was it because she and Milo had been talking about him? Was it because of what Milo said?

Probably some of all three. It didn't matter. It felt as if she was losing her mind.

No better place to do it than a little cottage in the middle of nowhere. If she started to scream and crawl the walls, nobody would be there to witness the meltdown of the century.

Summer would understand and would proceed to plan the funeral. They could have it at the end of the week, when she was back.

With her head on straight.

Maybe with a fish story—in Milo's honor.

Duke cocked his head and watched her closely as she dragged her suitcase out of the closet and started throwing clothes in it. Swimsuit. Shorts. Water shoes. A couple of summer dresses. Sandals. Some things to sleep in. Then she added toiletries and a lightweight jacket in case the evenings got cool. By this time, Duke was pacing, well aware that his routine was upset.

She dressed in jeans and a long-sleeved green T-shirt and slipped her feet into her favorite cowboy boots. Then she went to the kitchen, where she pulled out a half-full bag of dog food. Plenty for five days. She'd originally planned to leave on Sunday since the café was closed. But now she was free to leave a day early.

She pulled a sack out of the cupboard and haphazardly

picked items from her counters and cupboards. The half loaf of bread. A jar of peanut butter. Cereal. There had to be a small town nearby where she could buy milk. Two bottles of wine. She thought about adding another one but figured that was overkill. Boxes of macaroni and cheese. A jar of honey-roasted peanuts. And for the heck of it, she threw in the three bananas that she'd been ignoring for days.

She looked at her watch and debated whether she should call Summer now. Quickly discarded the idea. Summer had been so sick after seeing poor Milo's body. She needed her rest. Trish would call her in the morning to let her know her plans.

She made one more pass through her house, pausing outside her bedroom door to gaze at her pale gray bed skirt. Shaking her head, she walked into the room, got down on her knees, reached underneath the bed and pulled out her gun case.

Rafe had bought a gun for her several months after the last time she'd gone to the range with him. It had been a surprise. Initially she'd been inclined to tell him to take it back. But he'd been insistent. *You should have your own*, he'd said.

She hadn't shot it for more than four years. Had kept it locked up, under her bed. Was it crazy to pull it out now? M.A., who was single, had been traveling with her ten-year-old niece and she'd said that she'd felt perfectly safe.

But Trish wasn't a fool. She was a woman, traveling alone. A little extra protection made sense. Especially after what she'd seen earlier tonight.

She took it out of its case and slipped it into her shoulder bag. "Let's go," she said to Duke.

He followed her to the kitchen, and when she opened the door to her attached garage, he hurried ahead of her, like he always did. When she opened the passenger side door of her two-door Jeep, Duke jumped in and promptly scrambled over the middle console into the backseat. She went around back and shoved her suitcase and sack into the rear space. In the corner of her garage was her fishing gear. She grabbed it and put it in the Jeep. Then she got in.

Took a breath. Then another. Wiped her damp palms on her blue jeans.

She didn't normally steal away in the middle of the night.

But then, there had been nothing normal about this night. The heavy weight of her gun in her shoulder bag was even more proof of that.

It was just after one when she pulled out of the garage and shut the door behind her. Determined to think about something else, she turned on the radio and hunted for a station that had music. She finally found one that was playing oldies from the '50s and '60s.

Great. She felt about a hundred. It would be perfect.

She would be in the right area in just over an hour. It might take her a while to wind around the country roads and find the cottage. Hopefully her GPS would behave nicely.

"Are you excited?" she asked Duke.

He barked just once.

"I'll take that as a yes," she said, settling back. She wasn't worried about falling asleep while driving. Her body was practically humming with energy. She would not have been able to sleep.

She'd lost a good friend tonight.

Had Milo simply been a convenient target? Was it possible that a vagrant had been hiding in the alley, and when Milo had opened the door, the attack had been a spur-of-the-moment decision? Or was it something much more sinister? Had someone been waiting for Milo, someone from his past?

She prayed that Chase Hollister would find the answer. She wanted Milo's attacker to pay for what he'd done. It wouldn't bring Milo back but it would help to know that a killer had not gone free.

She pressed down on the accelerator, fully aware that she couldn't outrun the image of Milo's dead body on the dirty cement. She could not forget about what had happened. No. That was asking too much.

But she could drive, and then tomorrow, when she woke up in her little cottage, she would make coffee and take it down to the lake and dangle her feet in the cool water.

And she would come to terms with another senseless death.

She would have to.

Sometimes the only thing one could do was keep going.

RAFE GOT OFF the damn hill as fast as he could and ran the mile to where he'd hidden his car. Once inside, he sent a quick text to others on his team, letting them know about the arrival of the youngest Maladucci.

He looked at his watch, mindful of the seven-hour time difference between Italy and home. It was almost nine, which meant it was almost two in the morning at home. Time for most people to be sacked out.

But Daniel, who had sent this message, would be awake. He would anticipate that a return message was on its way.

He picked up his private cell phone. Trish? he typed and pushed Send.

Within minutes he had his response. Left café around midnight, arrived home safely.

He took a deep breath. Then another. That was good news. But he was edgy. Had been for the past twenty-four hours. Nothing unusual about that. Always the same, year after year.

Maybe someone was walking over his grave.

Hell, he'd walked over his own grave. Less than a month after Trish had the service, he'd been back in Ravesville, with Duke in tow. Just weeks before he'd died, he'd purchased the dog and arranged for it to be specially trained. From the beginning had called it Duke because Trish had always said that if she ever got a dog, Duke would be his name. His plan had been to surprise Trish on their one-year anniversary. When he'd had to leave, he'd expedited the training and delivered the dog to Trish's backyard two months earlier than expected.

But Duke had been a champ and Rafe had rested better knowing that the dog would protect Trish. Not that Trish should have been in danger still. That should have ended when Rafe left. But he couldn't stop being extra careful. Trish was too special.

So she'd been home for more than an hour. She would be sleeping. There was no need to request an updated report. No need at all.

Screw it. He typed. Reverify. And waited.

Thirteen minutes later, he knew something was terribly wrong when his phone rang. "Yeah," he answered.

"She's gone," Daniel said.

He gripped his phone and swallowed hard. "Signs of violence?"

"None. Dog is gone, too."

Milo was dead and Trish and Duke were missing. He stared up at the sun that was bright in the blue sky. It was going to be a nice day.

Not that it mattered. He had things to do.

IT WAS ALMOST two thirty before Trish pulled up in front of the cottage. There was a narrow half-gravel, half-grass road leading to the small wood structure. She knew the details from M.A. One bedroom, one bath, a kitchen and a big screened-in porch that had a great view of the water. It had sounded perfect, and now that she was here, even though it was too dark to see much of anything, she realized that she'd been right.

Unless, of course, there were mice inside. Even with her gun, she was no match for rodents. "Duke, you're going to need to protect me."

He nudged her shoulder with his wet nose. *I've got your back*, it seemed to say.

There was a small light burning next to the cottage door, but even as she walked the short distance from the car, she became aware of how dark the Missouri wilderness could be. Based on what M.A. had told her, the nearest cottage was a half mile away. It didn't help when Duke decided that he needed a potty break and he took his time sniffing for just the right area.

Her heart started to beat a little faster in her chest and she was glad when the dog finally finished. When it came time to enter the combination on the lock that hung over the door handle, she had to enter it twice before she got it right. The door swung open. Duke pushed in front of her and she made no effort to hold him back. She reached inside, hoping to feel for a light switch.

It was six inches farther away from the door than she'd expected. But once she found it and flipped the light on, she felt much better. It really was just perfect. The main part of the cottage had a small living area with just a couch and a bookshelf. There was no television. It led into the kitchen, where there was a big braided rug under the table. There was a stove, refrigerator and sink.

There was no door on what she suspected was the bedroom. She walked over and found the light. It had a double bed, a small table with a lamp and a dresser. The only other room in the main portion of the cottage was a small bathroom that was off the kitchen. It was old but clean with a bath/shower combination, a toilet and a vanity.

It was the porch that really interested her. It ran the entire length of the cottage, with windows and a back door making up one whole side. It was the size of all three of the other rooms put together. The shades on the windows and door were down, which made sense. She knew that she wouldn't be able to see anything right now anyway, but she was confident that in the morning, it was going to be dazzlingly beautiful. M.A. had told her the back door opened to steps that led to a long dock where the owner kept a boat for the renters to use. Then there was water for as far as you could see.

On the porch was a small, round slate table, the size where four could squeeze in to have breakfast, with four wrought-iron chairs with padded seats. Also a forest green sofa, a couple of overstuffed chairs, and a big wooden coffee table, the kind with drawers underneath. It had rained a couple of days when M.A. had been here and she'd said the board games and cards that she'd found in the coffee table had been a lifesaver.

Trish unpacked her sack, putting the few groceries

away in the cupboard. She pulled out Duke's water and food dishes and filled both. He immediately started eating.

It probably wasn't a bad idea. She'd had nothing since lunch, more than twelve hours earlier. She made herself a peanut butter and banana sandwich and poured a glass of water from the faucet. There was a roll of paper towels in a holder next to the sink. She pulled one off and wrapped it around her sandwich. Then she went onto the porch, sat on the sofa and ate.

It had been the right decision to come. She could feel it. Both her body and mind needed rest. Then she could face what had happened tonight.

She'd always figured that Rafe would have liked Milo. Would have appreciated the man's cooking ability, liked his dry sense of humor and been satisfied that he'd kept a watchful eye on Trish and Summer. Not that Ravesville was dangerous.

But it had been earlier tonight. She'd thought it couldn't get worse than when Summer's little girl had been kidnapped, along with her ex-husband. But she'd been wrong.

Murder.

She wadded up the paper towel around the quarter of the sandwich she hadn't eaten. Then got up, found the garbage container under the sink and tossed it away. Then she took her suitcase into the bedroom and opened it. Pajama pants and a tank were near the top and she quickly undressed and pulled them on.

Duke plopped down in the doorway, and she realized that without a door she'd probably be awakened the next morning, not by a hind-end knock, but rather by a lick in the face. "Maybe you should go outside again. You drank a lot of water."

His ears perked up.

"Let me get your leash," she said. She hadn't taken more than three steps when she heard a noise.

She listened. It had sounded like a car door. Not right outside but not far away, either.

Just one door.

At almost three in the morning.

"Could you hold it until morning?" she asked, absently rubbing the fur on Duke's back. She knew the dog was confused. He was starting to push up against her leg.

Maybe it was somebody else who was simply arriving at their cottage very late.

There was probably a very reasonable explanation for the noise.

She moved away from the door and Duke came with her. But instead of returning to her bedroom, she went back to the porch, detouring through the kitchen to get her shoulder bag. She pulled out her gun and sat on the sofa with her legs curled up underneath her.

This was crazy. Not counting the nine months that she'd lived with Rafe, she'd lived by herself since she was eighteen. Almost twenty years. She was independent. Certainly not someone who got spooked easily.

She'd also never had someone's blood on her knees before.

She listened carefully, didn't hear anything else. Minutes went by. She was almost ready to relax when she heard a noise outside the back door. Footsteps on what had to be the back steps that M.A. had described.

The hair on Duke's back stood up and she could see his teeth.

And then the knob on the back door started to turn.

She raised her gun.

Chapter Four

The locked door held. And the next sound she heard was a sharp knock.

She was surprised she heard it since her heart was beating so loudly. She didn't move. Duke continued his low growl.

"It's Bernie Wilberts. Is that you, Miss Roper?"

She almost dropped her gun. She managed to stuff it under the sofa cushion. Then she grabbed Duke's collar and hung on tight.

She recognized the voice. It was the man that she'd talked to on the telephone about renting the cottage.

She unlocked the door and opened it just inches. A man, his body lean and tall, with a few lines on his tanned face, stood on the back porch. He had a flashlight but it was pointed down toward the ground. He looked interested, but not terribly alarmed that he'd encountered someone in a cottage that was supposed to be empty.

"Hi," she said. "Yes, I'm Trish Wright-Roper. I arrived early."

"I saw the car and figured that was the case. And then I saw the light, so I figured I better check."

She opened the door a little wider. "You're out late,

Mr. Wilberts. I was going to call you but I didn't want to interrupt your sleep."

"Call me Bernie," he said. "I wasn't even Mr. Wilberts when I was in the corporate world. Anyway, best fishing is in the middle of the night."

That made her think about Milo and what had sent her scrambling to the cottage. He'd caught his last bass. She felt a pain in her chest and wondered when it would get easier. "Of course," she said.

By now, Duke had squirmed his way around her legs and poked his nose out the door.

"That's a fine-looking dog," Bernie said.

"He was just about to go out," she said. "Duke, sit." The dog, who normally obeyed really well, continued to pull forward, and she knew that she was about to lose her grip.

"Watch out," she said.

Duke flew past Bernie, almost knocking the man off the back steps. *Oh, good grief*, she thought, stepping out after him. Her bare feet hit the back step. There was just enough room for her and Bernie. "Sorry about that," she said.

She could hear Duke, thrashing around, but couldn't see him. It was very dark outside. "May I?" she said, pointing at Bernie's flashlight.

"Of course," he said.

She shone the light around and caught a glimpse of Duke. He was circling a log. "Get busy, Duke," she called out, her voice soft, aware that even though there weren't any close neighbors, sound carried at night.

"Looks as if he could hold his own against the coyotes," Bernie said.

That didn't scare her. She'd had coyotes in her backyard for years. But even so, she hoped the dog had the good sense to come back in. She didn't relish looking for him in the dark.

Duke came bounding back onto the steps and she stepped back inside. "Well, I'll be going, then," Bernie said. "I'll stop back at a more reasonable time tomorrow or the next day, and we can get acquainted."

"Great," she said. "I'll be interested in learning about the best fishing spots."

She watched the man walk down the steps and around the corner of the cottage, presumably toward a car that he'd parked somewhere nearby. She shut and locked the door.

She turned and looked at Duke. "Well, that was exciting," she said.

He barked once in response.

She turned off the light on the porch. "We made the right decision, Duke," she said. "We needed this."

BERNIE WILBERTS DIALED the number that he knew by heart. "She's there," he said. "Early."

"Why?"

"How the hell should I know?" He hated this. He really did. "I saw a car and I checked. She's by herself. She's got a dog. But I suspect a bullet will take care of him easy enough."

The voice at the other end was quiet for a moment. "Fine. I'll be in touch."

IT WAS CLOSE to nine before Trish woke up. Given that it had been after four before she'd dropped off, she knew she could probably have slept later. But Duke had other ideas when he put his nose in her face.

"Fine," she muttered, throwing back the sheet.

He ran to the door and then had to wait for her. She walked, scuffing her bare feet on the wood floor. Running was out of the question until she'd had coffee. She snapped on his leash and opened the front door. She took a few steps outside and let the leash out so the dog would have his choice of trees and shrubs to water.

She could hear birds singing in the trees and there wasn't a cloud in the blue sky. It was a perfect day.

She took a deep breath. Then another, expanding her lungs. The air was already warm and was heavy with humidity. The trees smelled damp and she knew it had rained here recently. There was mud around the log that Duke was once again circling.

If he got dirty, he could wash off in the lake. She might do the same.

However, he managed to stay clean, and once he was done, they went back inside. She checked her cell phone to see if there were calls from Summer. Thankfully there were not. She would have been worried if Trish had not answered.

She dialed her and it rang three times before Summer picked up. "Hey," her twin said. "I was just about to call you."

"How are you feeling?" Trish asked.

"Better," Summer said. "I'm sorry I couldn't stay last night."

"If you hadn't voluntarily left, I think Bray might have had a stroke."

"He worries," Summer said. "I've tried to tell him that I threw up every day for three months when I was pregnant with Keagan and Adie, but he's not buying it."

Her sister was very lucky. She and Bray had loved

each other since they were teenagers, but life had intervened and it had taken them fifteen years to find their way to one another.

"I need a favor," Trish said.

"Of course."

"Can you take care of the arrangements for Milo's service? I would help but I drove to the Ozarks last night."

"In the middle of the night?" Summer squeaked.

Trish almost laughed. "Yes, Mother. In the middle of the night. But I arrived safe and sound. No need to worry. And speaking of mothers, will you let Mom know what's going on?"

"Of course. But where are you?"

"Near Heelie Lake. I got a recommendation from M.A. She was here recently with her niece. You knew I'd been planning to take a few days off once you were back. After this thing with Milo, I thought about canceling, but I…I just had to get away."

"I totally get it. It's so awful. I'm going to miss him so much."

She could tell Summer was close to tears.

"I'll be back on Wednesday."

"Promise me that you'll keep your cell phone on and charged at all times. And no more driving in the middle of the night."

"Of course," Trish said.

There was a pause on the other end. Finally, Summer spoke. "It must be horrible for you, Trish. To have Milo die on the same day as Rafe. It's just too much."

"Two good men," Trish said, her own throat closing up.

"I'm glad you got away," Summer said. "I'm really glad. Just be safe. I love you. We all do."

The line went dead. And Trish knew her twin was either crying or vomiting. But Bray would be there to handle either.

Maybe if she'd had someone at home, someone to hold her, she wouldn't have felt the need to run in the middle of the night. She didn't begrudge her twin's happiness. Their lives were just different and she'd learned a long time ago to accept that.

She put her cell phone down and started a pot of coffee. Then she raised every shade on the porch, even the one on the door. M.A. had been right. The view was lovely. From the back steps, there was a little patch of grass that M.A. hadn't mentioned, maybe twenty feet wide, before one hit the edge of the water.

The wooden dock that extended another fifty feet over the water was faded but in good repair. Bernie Wilberts's boat, tied at the end, was white with brown panels. The aluminum fishing boat wasn't new but, like the dock, appeared sturdy. It would suit her just fine.

Now that the blinds were up, she realized that wasn't enough. She opened several of the windows, happy to see that there were screens to keep the bugs out. Duke rested his chin on one of the sills, looking about as happy as a dog could look.

She could practically hear the lake calling her name. *Trish. Trish Wright-Roper.*

"Give me ten minutes," she said to Duke.

She walked back into the kitchen, toasted two slices of bread and slathered them with peanut butter. She grabbed a couple of handfuls of dry cereal and chewed. She washed it all down with the coffee that was now ready.

She hadn't bothered to unpack the night before. But now she opened her suitcase and pulled out light blue capri pants and a blue-and-white tank. She slipped on a pair of sandals that she'd brought. She loved her cowboy boots but they weren't good for dangling feet in the water.

On her way out the back door, she grabbed a well-read romance novel off the bookshelf in the living room. Duke bounded ahead of her, racing up and down the dock three times before she made it to the end.

The sun was warm on her face and she could smell the heady scent of the water. There was very little algae and, when she sat at the very end of the dock, it was clear enough that she could see the bottom of the lake through the ten or so feet of water.

Two hours later, she was a hundred and thirty-eight pages into her book, pleasantly warm and, truth be told, a little sleepy. But there were things she needed to do. The idea of more dry cereal was not appealing. She needed to find a grocery store. It was a little early for lunch but she wasn't on anybody's schedule but her own. She'd grab a bite to eat and still have the whole afternoon to take the boat out for a little fishing. Bernie Wilberts might like to dangle a line in the middle of the night. Not her.

She stood up and Duke, who had been stretched out next to her sleeping in the sun, immediately woke up. He stayed close as she walked back to the cottage. Once inside, she tossed her book on the slate table and then closed and locked all the windows and did the same for the back door.

Then she grabbed her purse and keys and walked out the front door, making sure that it was locked behind her. She opened up the door of her Jeep and Duke jumped in.

It was fifteen minutes before she got to Heelie. She

wasn't sure which had come first. The town or the lake. But now each was an extension of the other. Every other place on the three-block stretch was a T-shirt shop or a souvenir store. There was one coffee shop, three ice cream parlors and two small restaurants. She parked in front of one. She rolled down the window for Duke. She wasn't worried about anybody stealing him. He'd bite the person's arm off who tried that.

The place had fewer tables than the Wright Here, Wright Now Café and there was no shiny pie case in the corner. The menu looked similar but the prices were higher.

Maybe it was time for her and Summer to increase theirs. She ordered a BLT with fries and, to test the young waitress, an Arnold Palmer to drink. The girl smiled and said, "My mom drinks those."

Trish managed to keep a smile on her face as the young girl trotted off to get her lemonade–iced tea combination. The girl's comment had been a stark reminder that she was an age where she could have a daughter working behind the counter.

But look at Summer, a little voice nagged at her, as she unrolled and rerolled her silverware, tighter than it had been before. Summer was exactly the same age and she'd be having a new baby in seven months.

You're not over the hill, she told herself.

But had she crested the peak and was the descent staring her in the face? Suddenly motivated, she pulled out her smartphone and scanned her emails, looking for the last one from the guy that she'd met online. The one she'd told Milo about.

Maybe it was time to fish or cut bait.

Barry North wanted to meet her for dinner. She found

his message and, before she could change her mind, sent him a quick note confirming that she'd be available to meet him the following Saturday.

When her BLT and fries arrived, she forced herself to eat. She was moving on. This was good. When she got back to Ravesville, she was tossing out those self-help books about dealing with loss. She was dealing just fine.

She'd just pushed her plate away when her phone dinged, indicating a new email. She picked it up, ignoring that her hand was shaking. So great to get your message. Glad we're finally going to do this. Where and when? I don't mind a drive.

She'd told him that she lived about ninety minutes south-west of St. Louis but hadn't been specific about Ravesville. She wasn't stupid. She might be new at the online dating game, but she knew enough not to give out her personal information. He lived in Kansas City.

Maybe Hamerton. It was a twenty-minute drive from Ravesville. There were a couple of good places there. She wanted someplace nice but not too fancy. She typed back. Mulder's in Hamerton. At seven.

Almost immediately came the response. Looking forward to it.

She closed her phone feeling suddenly very warm. She had a date. The idea of it made her BLT rumble in her stomach.

She pushed her chair back, walked to her Jeep and got Duke out to take a little stroll. They went up and down the streets, with Duke stopping frequently to drink out of the dog water bowls that many of the merchants left outside their entrances.

Then it was back to the Jeep for Duke while she went to the grocery store and bought milk and eggs and more fresh vegetables than she probably needed. But hopefully she'd catch a fish this afternoon and be able to cook the fish and the vegetables on the gas grill that was chained outside the cottage.

Back at the Jeep, she shoved the groceries inside the back door and slipped into the driver's seat. It was a very warm day, and through her capri pants, she could feel the heat of the leather. She leaned back in the seat gingerly, knowing that her tank wouldn't provide much protection. She'd pulled her hair into a low ponytail, like she usually wore it to work, but it felt heavy on her neck. Maybe it would be cooler on the water.

She checked both ways and then pulled out of her parking space. Duke had his head hanging out the window. There was a lot of traffic that didn't lighten up until she'd turned off onto the side road that would wind around until it led her to the cottage.

She remembered several of the hairpin turns from the previous night and realized that they were much scarier in the daytime. She hadn't been able to see how narrow the shoulder on the road was.

Fifteen minutes later, when she was back at the cottage, she let Duke out to do his thing and grabbed the groceries. She held both plastic bags in one hand so that she had a free hand to enter the combination.

She got it on the first try this time. The door swung open.

And by habit, her eyes swept the room. Call her crazy but it seemed different than it had when she'd left two hours earlier. It smelled different. And the handle of the faucet on the kitchen sink was turned to a slightly different angle. And the rug on the floor had one corner flipped up, as if someone had caught it with a shoe.

Trust your instincts.

She could almost hear Rafe's voice in her ear.

She dropped her groceries and ran for her car. Where the hell was Duke?

She was reaching for the Jeep door when someone caught her from behind. She turned, swinging her fist.

The stranger caught her arm. He was big and beefy and he smelled strongly of garlic. He was completely bald, maybe late fifties.

She opened her mouth to scream and he backhanded her. She fell to her knees.

"Shut up or we put a bullet in you," he said. "Get the dog."

She thought he was talking to her but realized that there was a second man. He was standing five feet away, holding a gun. He was much younger, with dark hair that touched his shoulders. But there was no doubt that the two were related, maybe father and son.

Her ears were ringing and she was pretty sure she had a bloody nose. She lifted her head, looking for Duke. He was fifty feet away, his fur raised, on full alert. He was going to charge the man with the gun.

"Oh, no, Duke," she cried.

The man pulled the trigger, catching Duke as he leaped into the air. She heard his sharp yelp of pain and saw him fall.

Duke's big body hit the hard ground and he lay there.

She pushed herself off the ground. She had to help him. "You bastard," she screamed. "You killed him."

And when the younger man laughed, Trish launched herself in his direction, kicking and screaming with everything she had.

It took both men to subdue her, and she only stopped

when they had her on the ground with the gun pressed up against her temple. She turned her head to see her poor dog.

He lay absolutely still.

Chapter Five

"You son of a bitch," she screamed at the younger man.

He laughed and yanked her arm, pulling her to a standing position. Then he pushed her toward the cottage and through the doorway. She stumbled over the spilled groceries. She was shoved toward a kitchen chair and her tailbone hit it hard.

The older man had followed them in and was now going through her purse that she'd dropped outside during the struggle. He pulled out her billfold, flipped it open and held it up, squinting at it. "Trish Wright-Roper. Jackpot."

He had to be comparing her to her driver's license. Jackpot. That could mean only one thing. This hadn't happened by chance. They'd been looking for her.

It made no sense. She didn't have enemies.

Maybe not, but a man had been murdered outside her café the previous night. Was that what this was about? Milo?

She sat in the chair and faced her attackers, attempting to control her spiking emotions. The idea that these men might have had something to do with Milo's death fueled an anger that she'd never thought herself capable of. And then there was what they'd done to poor Duke.

But she couldn't get so upset that she couldn't think.

"Anthony, go finish off that dog," the older man said.

He pulled Trish's cell phone out of her purse. He didn't bother to look at it. Just dropped it on the ground and stepped on it with the heel of his boot.

Anthony looked up from the cookies he'd grabbed from the floor. He tore at the packaging. "I'm eating."

"You can eat when this is over," the older man said. He spoke in a tone that made it clear he considered himself in charge.

Anthony evidently understood the pecking order because he tossed the now-open cookies onto the counter. "What the hell am I supposed to do with it?"

"This isn't that difficult. Just get it out of sight. Put the carcass in the woods, under something."

Duke deserved so much more. She was going to kill both of these men when she had the chance. And leave their bodies for the buzzards.

Anthony stalked to the door, leaving it open behind him. She couldn't see but Old Guy was watching.

"What?" he said loudly, his voice cross.

Anthony didn't answer, but perhaps he motioned or something because a look of exasperation crossed Old Guy's face. "Fine," he said. "Just come back in."

She could barely keep the smile off her face. It could mean only one thing. Duke had somehow had enough life in him to slink away.

Stay alive, Duke, she thought. *I'll try to do the same.* With that thought in mind, she once again tried to channel her anger, to make it into something productive. Her phone was out of commission but her gun was still on the porch, still stuffed underneath the cushion, where she'd left it last night. She needed to somehow find a way to get to it.

When Anthony came back inside, he picked up the

other groceries on the floor and seemed delighted that the eggs hadn't broken. He ignored the cookies he'd opened and poured himself a bowl of cereal. He added milk and noisily ate. Old Guy gave him a dirty look but didn't say anything else.

"Who are you?" she asked, proud that her voice didn't shake. She would not let these people know that she was terrified.

"Why, we have friends in common," said Old Guy. Then he laughed and wiped his sweaty brow with the back of his hand. "That makes us friends."

She was confident that she'd never seen either of these two men before. But she decided to let his comment play out. "You've got an odd way of showing it," she said.

He shrugged and turned his head to look at Anthony. "Tie her up."

Anthony set down his bowl and pulled out a small ball of heavy twine from his pants pocket. He squatted in front of her. He smelled of sweat and garlic and she fought back the urge to gag. When he roughly pulled her ankles together and wrapped the twine around four times and then tied it tight, she fought back the instinct to scream.

"To the chair," Old Guy said, frowning.

Anthony stood up. Instead of tying her wrists together, he tied each wrist to the back of the chair, at the spot where the seat curved down to the leg.

If she went anywhere, the chair was going with her.

"Now what?" she asked.

"Now we wait," said Old Guy, smiling at her.

"For?" Trish asked. She needed to figure out the plan if she hoped to outthink them.

His smile faded. "Stop asking questions or I'll gag you. You'll know soon enough."

He pulled a cell phone out of his shirt pocket. Held it up so that he could take a picture of her. Evidently not happy with the shot, he moved to the side. "Anthony," he said, motioning for the man. "Put your gun up to her temple."

Anthony seemed only too happy to do that. She could feel it, warm from either the sun or the man's body, pressing against the soft part of her skull.

Old Guy took several shots. Then he lowered the phone and typed something, using his thumb. "That should do it," he said.

Were they sending the picture to Summer? Trish's stomach twisted at the idea of her sister opening up a message and seeing this. It had been only six months since Adie had been kidnapped. Could Summer survive this again?

She could. She was strong. And now she had Bray and his brothers, too. They would find her. Save her. She had to hold on to that thought.

"He won't be able to resist that," Old Guy said.

He? He who?

But Old Guy was done talking. He walked out onto the porch and she lost her view of him. But she could hear him cross the length of the porch, heard a creak as he sat down. Probably on the couch. Maybe even on the same cushion that her gun was stuffed under. She guessed it was too much to hope for that it would accidentally go off and shoot him.

But Old Guy didn't worry her as much as Anthony, who was staring at her. With her arms behind her back, her breasts were more prominent, pushing against the thin material of her tank top.

If he touched her, that would be more than she could endure.

AFTER LEAVING THE MALADUCCIS', Rafe drove to his apartment and picked up the things he would need. On the way to the Milan airport, he made phone calls. One to Henri, to let him know that his services were going to be needed.

Nobody knew about Henri. Rafe had encountered the man years before he'd ever met Trish. It had set him back some to look across a crowded restaurant and see someone who very closely resembled him. It was widely believed that everybody had a double. Well, Rafe had met his.

He'd cultivated a relationship with Henri that had been profitable to both of them. Financially profitable for Henri because Rafe paid him very well. Rafe had benefited from the resemblance because whenever Rafe was supposedly off the clock on holiday, Henri filled in, coming and going from Rafe's apartment, making it appear as if Rafe was indeed home.

Truth be told, Rafe had actually been in the United States, spying on his wife. Nobody that he worked with knew about Trish. Not even his boss. And he intended to keep it that way. It was safer for her.

Once Rafe had been confident that Henri understood the plan, he'd made a second call to arrange transport back to St. Louis. He didn't intend to fly commercial. First of all, there were no direct flights from Milan to St. Louis. He would have to connect in New York or Atlanta and there would likely be delay after delay.

And he didn't intend for his name to show on any manifest. At least, not yet. That was essential.

For years, he'd prepared to have to make a last-minute flight back to the States. Just in case. That was going to pay off today.

His call was answered. He spoke in the common language of dollars and, within five minutes, had secured a spot on a charter flight that, according to the manifest, was delivering medical equipment. Perhaps there would be an antiseptic wipe on board.

He was leaving at 10:00 a.m. his time, which was 3:00 a.m. Missouri time. It was a ten-hour flight. Therefore, he would be there by 1:00 p.m. Missouri time. He sent a text to Daniel to let him know where to pick him up.

He parked his car, walked up the steps of the plane, spoke to the pilot briefly and settled into his seat. He listened to the engines rev up as the plane taxied down the runway and tried to tell himself that there could be a thousand reasons why Trish wasn't at her house. It did not mean she was in trouble.

After all, she'd taken Duke with her. That was a good sign. Right?

But somebody had killed Milo. It was possible that it had been random. Even so, it was plenty enough to get his attention and to get him back to the States. The timing was bad but he'd stay just long enough to ensure that Trish was okay.

He slept on the plane, not because he was terribly tired, but because he knew that it might be a while before he could sleep again.

Trish was missing. Once his feet hit the ground, he would not stop until he knew she was safe.

The plane landed about twenty minutes early. At the pilot's signal, Rafe lifted the hatch on the floor of the plane and dropped down into the cargo hold. Then he got into the empty crate and pulled the door shut. He had to wait several long minutes before he heard the sound of a door. Then he hung on while a forklift off-loaded him and his crate.

Fifteen minutes later, he heard a click and the door of the crate popped open. He pushed his head out. He was on a dock. Nobody around. He exited and calmly walked to the front of the warehouse. A blast of warm air hit his face. It took him a minute to figure out where he was and then he sent a quick text to Daniel.

It was just after 1:00 p.m. It would be 8:00 in Italy. The Maladuccis would have finished their predinner cocktails and be sitting down for the meal.

His phone pinged and he thought it was probably Daniel responding. He glanced at it and almost stepped off the curb in front of an oncoming semi. Trish. Oh, God. Tied up. With a gun to her head. Blood on her face. Her shirt. His hands shook as he studied the photo.

The message below the picture was brief. We'll trade her for you.

Chapter Six

With a few clicks, Rafe ran the text message through software on his phone. But it couldn't be traced. He was able to tell that the picture had been taken two minutes ago.

He texted back. He wanted to beg them not to hurt her, to tell them that he'd do anything. Instead, he typed, I'm willing to talk.

The reply came immediately. Come to Missouri. Further instruction will be sent.

He heard the sharp tap of a horn and looked up into the eyes of his trusted friend. He and Daniel had gone to college together and stayed good friends ever since. Daniel had joined the FBI years ago and was the most accomplished man that Rafe had ever met. He had a pilot's license and flew his own plane. He had scuba dived the great reefs of the world and he spoke five or six languages fluently.

He was also a chameleon, and when there had been a concern that the Ravesville police chief was involved in significant illegal activity, some of which had involved the transportation of minors across state lines, the FBI had sent him to Ravesville to play the role of small-town police officer.

It was years after Rafe had left Ravesville but still

fortuitous because it had given him another set of eyes besides Milo to watch over Trish.

With Chief Poole in jail and Chase Hollister now occupying that chair, there had been no need for Daniel's continued service in Ravesville. He was currently working out of the Chicago FBI office but he kept his ear to the ground for Rafe, passing along tidbits that he heard.

Rafe got into the car. Showed the man the text. Daniel let loose with several words that Rafe had wanted to say. He was holding his emotions in. Barely.

"Well, I guess now we know," Daniel said, finishing up. "I'm sorry, Rafe."

"I know." He was sorry, too, and more angry than he'd ever been in his whole life. But none of that did them any good. "Thank you for letting me know about Milo. How did you hear?"

"I monitor the Twitter and Facebook pages of several men on the volunteer fire department. One of them Tweeted that the cook at the Wright Here, Wright Now Café had been murdered. I got to the airport as quickly as I could, flew here and managed to arrive a half hour before Trish drove herself home, followed by Bray Hollister."

If Daniel hadn't alerted Rafe about Milo's death and then subsequently confirmed that Trish was missing from her apartment, he'd have been totally surprised by the picture of her. He'd probably have had a damn heart attack. Even now, with ten-plus hours to have anticipated the worst, it had still been pretty horrific to see that photo.

"Do you have any idea who is behind this?" Daniel asked.

"No, not for sure. I've always believed that Luciano Maladucci was behind the *accidents* that happened to my colleagues. If I had to guess, it would be him. Maybe they got tipped off that I'm getting close again."

"You need to know something. I didn't know this when I gave you the news about Milo."

"What?"

"Milo had some poignant last words. 'Tell Rafe they know.' I talked to Chase Hollister this morning. He told me to see if it possibly meant anything to me."

"What did you tell him?"

"Told him I had no idea."

"Who did Milo say this to?"

"Trish. She found him."

The news settled on him, almost taking his breath away. Trish should never have to see things like that. It wasn't the world she lived in. And what the hell would she have thought hearing those words? Maybe she'd been in such shock that the words hadn't really registered. Hadn't meant anything.

They meant something to him. Milo had wanted to warn him that danger was closing in. It had to be big. Nothing else would have made Milo sacrifice the truth. *Tell Rafe.* By that, he had opened the door that Rafe Roper might not really be dead. He'd protected the secret for a long time. Even dying, he wouldn't have said it if it wasn't vitally important.

As they pulled away from the curb, Rafe pulled out a second phone from his shirt pocket. He scanned the numbers. There were only just a handful in this particular phone. He pressed the one he wanted. "Go," he said when the phone was answered. Then he hung up.

He settled back in his seat. Right now, if they were tracking his accounts, and he assumed they were, they would see him online, purchasing a seat on a charter flight that in one hour would fly him from Milan, Italy, to the St. Louis airport. Next, they would see him arrange for a rental car in St. Louis.

If they had someone at the airport, and he suspected they would, they would know when his passport and boarding pass were scanned. His seat would be occupied. By Henri. Once the plane landed in St. Louis, he suspected that was when further instruction would arrive.

It was a ten-hour flight. The plane would land in St. Louis at midnight.

It was 1:00 p.m. now. That meant he had eleven hours to find Trish before they thought his feet were touching US soil.

He glanced at his phone, at the picture. Even bloody and bound, she was still so beautiful. So perfect in every way.

It had almost killed him to leave her. But he knew that it was the only way to protect her. They would have found him eventually. Discovered Trish. Known that the easiest way to make him pay for what he'd done to them was to hurt her.

So Rafe Roper had died.

He glanced at Daniel. "Is there anything else?"

He shook his head. "Summer and Bray Hollister were at the funeral home this morning, making arrangements for Milo. They did not appear to be distressed."

That wasn't good. It meant that Trish had probably made some kind of contact with Summer before she'd been apprehended. They weren't worried about her, wouldn't be looking for her.

But it also meant that they might have some idea of where she was. So, in order to find out where Trish was, he was going to have to go through Summer or her new husband. He'd done his research on Bray Hollister when the man had first come back to Ravesville. He'd been a DEA agent and had built a reputation as being tough as nails. He'd still be easier to talk to than Summer, who would want to skin him alive.

He opened his contacts on his telephone and found Bray Hollister's number. It had been in his phone for months. He started typing. When he finished, his message said, Need to meet. Come alone. 2nd floor, across from café. In 90 minutes.

Based on what he knew about Bray Hollister, he'd come. And he probably wouldn't tell his new bride—he wouldn't want to worry her needlessly. But he wasn't stupid. He'd have one or both of his brothers as backup. Fine. Might as well get it over with. They were a tight group, those Hollister brothers, based on what he'd heard.

In five minutes, he got a return text. Who is this? Who gave you this number?

I will explain. Milo gave it to me.

There were no other texts from Bray. He hoped that meant the man would be there to meet him when they rolled into Ravesville.

It was a bright, sunny afternoon, far different than the first night he'd rolled into Ravesville. The light had been fading fast when he'd heard the sounds of the tornado siren. He'd looked off to his left and he was pretty sure he could see the makings of a funnel cloud.

But still, he'd have tried to outrun it. If he hadn't looked through that damn window of the Wright Here, Wright Now Café and seen the most beautiful woman ever. She was tall and fit and had silky red hair to her waist.

And he decided it wouldn't be a bad idea to wait out the storm in her company. He figured it might be a couple of hours of fun and, if he got real lucky, maybe an hour of sweaty sex.

But somewhere in the middle of his second piece of banana cream pie, he realized that he was in trouble. This woman was different. This woman could make him want things that he couldn't have.

This woman was meant to be his.

And so he'd broken his own rules and hoped like hell that it would be okay. And it was better than okay. It was damn near perfect until he'd got the first call. Then the second. The team was dropping like flies. Somebody had flipped on them.

He didn't know whom he could trust.

So he'd done the only thing he could do.

But now Milo was dead.

Another death.

This time he would settle it and settle it for good. But first he had to find Trish, make sure she was safe.

EIGHTY-ONE MINUTES LATER they entered Ravesville. "I'll walk from here," Rafe said. "I'll need a vehicle."

"It'll be parked a block east. A black BMW."

"Thank you." Once he knew where Trish was, he'd be on the road again. "I appreciate your help."

Daniel smiled. "I hope it works out for you and Trish. I really do. I'll stick around Ravesville for a few days in the event you need me."

Rafe got out and walked the two blocks to the building across from the café. When he rounded the corner of the second floor, he saw that Bray Hollister had got there early. He was lounging against the wall, his stance casual.

"Thank you for coming," Rafe said.

Bray didn't respond.

Rafe already had the keys in his hand. He hadn't wanted to have to pull them out of his pocket—Hollister might get nervous and shoot him with the gun that he was sure to be wearing.

He kept his hands where Hollister could see them and turned to open the door. He walked into the empty apartment, turned and stood with his back against the wall. "There's nobody else here," he said.

Hollister must have believed him because he followed him in and shut the door.

"My name is Rafe Roper," he said.

Hollister considered him. Finally, he spoke. "You son of a bitch. Trish thinks you're dead."

"It's a long story," he said. "But right now, I need to know where Trish is. She could be in danger."

That got Hollister's attention. "From who?"

"From the people who killed Milo," Rafe said. He didn't intend to show Hollister the text message. Based on what he'd been told about the man, there was no way that he was going to leave law enforcement out of it.

And Rafe didn't know whom he could trust.

Hollister was either a really good actor or he really wasn't a bit surprised that Trish's trouble had something to do with Milo. He undoubtedly had heard about Milo's last words and he was piecing the information together.

Hollister walked over to the window, pulled back the curtain. "I saw you up here. It was around Thanksgiving. You were watching the café."

That had been the last time he'd been in the States. And he had been in Ravesville. But to the best of his knowledge, nobody had ever seen him watching over the café. "You're observant," Rafe said. "I was already on my way out of the country before I heard about Adie's disappearance. I was glad to hear that things worked out okay."

Hollister turned to look at him. "Milo had some last words. For Trish."

Rafe waited.

"He said, 'Tell Rafe they know.'"

He pretended to be surprised. No need for them to start looking at Daniel.

"Who's behind this?" Hollister demanded.

"I don't know." But if it was the people he thought, they'd killed before and were coming back to finish the job.

"Where's Trish?" Rafe asked.

"Who do you work for?" Hollister demanded.

"It's better that you don't know," Rafe said. "But I am no threat to you or your family."

"Of course you are. You just told me Trish was in danger."

"I'll handle this."

Hollister didn't look convinced but he gave up on the line of questioning fairly easily. He had probably figured out that no amount of asking was going to get Rafe to tell him anything else. "You do realize that when you find Trish you're going to have a whole lot of explaining to do," Hollister said. "I'm going to assume you left her for the right reasons. But even that might not make a difference."

He was prepared for that. It would hurt him badly but nothing was more important than finding Trish and keeping her safe. "Where is she?"

"I know an approximate location," Hollister said. "When she talked to Summer, she said she was at a cottage near Heelie Lake in the Ozarks."

"Address?" Rafe said, pulling out his phone.

"She didn't give Summer one. But she did say that the cottage had been recommended by a woman who eats in the café. M.A. Fikus."

The name meant nothing to Rafe. He keyed in information on his phone. Within minutes, he knew Mary Ann Fikus was single, worked at the Ravesville bank and had a peanut allergy. On her social media pages, she talked about making quilts and apple butter.

He kept flipping screens until he had her street address. That was where he was headed next. He put his phone back in his pocket and walked over to the door. "Hollister, will you come with me to M.A.'s house? She might not be willing to tell me anything but she knows you."

Steady eyes studied him. "You can call me Bray," he said. "After all, I think we're sort of family."

In his world, the luxury of family had always been beyond his reach. "Thank you," he said.

The BMW was exactly where it was supposed to be. He got in it and Bray followed him in his own vehicle. They pulled up in front of M.A. Fikus's house within four minutes. He was anxious to meet the woman, get the information and get on the road.

He could hear the music from the sidewalk. M.A. liked badass rock and roll and she liked it loud. That didn't fit the image he had of the quilter and apple butter maker.

He was still three feet away from the front door when he saw that it was open and the lock had been broken, as if somebody had taken a foot to the door. He pulled his gun and confirmed that Bray was indeed carrying when suddenly there was a gun in his hand, too.

The two men entered the living room. There was no

sign of distress. He motioned to Bray that he was going to look right. Bray went the opposite direction.

It was a small house, just two bedrooms and one bath. It didn't take him long. He'd just finished the bath when he heard Bray Hollister.

"Rafe, back porch."

M.A. was dressed in workout clothes but she wasn't going to have to ever worry about her weight again. She was on her stomach and she'd been shot in the back three times.

It was possible that she'd never even known that an intruder was in her house.

"Call it in," Rafe said. "You can tell your brother I was here but I'd appreciate it if my name wasn't in the police report."

"How are you going to find Trish now?"

"M.A.'s bank records. Credit card receipts. If she recently stayed there, I should be able to narrow the area fairly quickly."

"You have access to all that?"

"I do," he said simply. "Does she have family?" he asked, looking at the woman.

"I'm not sure. Summer will know."

"If there are…issues with money, you know, for paying for the funeral, I'll take care of it," he said, already moving for the door.

"Rafe," Bray said, stopping him. "Be careful. If you really get yourself killed out there this time, Trish will never forgive either one of us." He held up a finger. "And you better be as good as I suspect you are. Because if you fail and I have to tell Summer that something has happened to Trish, I'm going to hunt you down and rip out your heart."

Chapter Seven

It took Rafe less than twenty minutes to piece together M.A. Fikus's last vacation. She'd bought gas, groceries and a sub sandwich in Heelie. Had got a massage there, too. That had occurred the day after she'd rented a kayak at a marina at Heelie Lake.

Banking records told a story. Unfortunately, there were no transactions for lodging.

What role did M.A. play in all of this? Was she simply an acquaintance of Trish's who happened to mention a great vacation spot? Was she an unwitting accomplice and she'd been duped into leading Trish away from the safety of Ravesville? Had she been one of them? And had something gone terribly wrong that she'd had to be culled from the group?

So many questions but at least he had someplace to begin. He started his car, knowing that he'd be in the right area in a little more than an hour.

He would find Trish.

And then he was going to break the bastards who'd hurt her.

TRISH'S SHOULDERS HURT from being pulled back and her lower back ached like hell from having her spine arched.

The only good thing was that Anthony had left her alone in the kitchen. He had gone into her bedroom and, by the sounds of the creaking springs, was taking a nap on her bed. He'd turned on the radio next to the bed and she could hear sounds of a ball game.

Everyday stuff.

Except she was tied up. Waiting.

For who?

She wished she'd thought to tell Summer that she'd check in later during the day. If she had done that, and the call didn't come, Summer would send the cavalry. But now she would have no idea that Trish was in trouble.

It really was up to her.

Unless she got lucky and Bernie Wilberts decided to show up. But truthfully, she didn't really want that. He was a nice guy who would be quickly overpowered by these two and then she'd have someone else to save besides herself.

She decided it was time to see how much leverage she might have. "Hey," she said. "I have to go to the bathroom."

There was no answer.

"Hey," she said again. "I really do."

"Anthony," boomed the voice from the porch.

Anthony didn't answer. She suspected he was sound asleep because she was pretty confident that the baseball announcer wasn't the one snoring.

She heard noise on the porch and then Old Guy walked around the corner. He glanced into the bedroom and shook his head in disgust. But he didn't wake Anthony up. Instead, he pulled a pocketknife from his pants, extending the blade, and cut her arms and feet loose. "Out in two minutes or I'm coming in to get you."

She didn't waste any time getting to the bathroom and shutting the door. She used the toilet because she really did have to go. Then hurriedly washed her hands and face, scrubbing the dried blood off. Her nose hurt but she didn't think it was broken.

She glanced around the room, hoping for some kind of weapon. There was nothing. Not even a damn razor. She hadn't planned on shaving her legs while she was here. And there was no window in the bathroom.

She opened the door. Old Guy had taken her chair. He got up and motioned for her to sit down.

"Could I have some water, please," she said.

He shrugged.

She took that for a yes. She opened a cupboard door and pulled out a glass. Ran the water. Filled the glass half-full and drank it.

She needed to get to the porch. Her gun was less than twenty feet away but it might as well be on the moon if she couldn't find a reason to get out there. "I'm cold," she said. "Can I get that blanket off the sofa on the porch?" she asked, already starting to cross the kitchen.

He moved fast, grabbing her arm and swinging her around. "You ain't going nowhere," he said. He shoved her down into the chair and picked up the twine.

She automatically got into the position that Anthony had tied her in the first time. Old Guy wrapped the twine even tighter than Anthony had and it cut into her skin.

But she was still happy. Because when she'd got her glass of water, she'd seen the key to Bernie Wilberts's boat next to the toaster. And she'd come up with a plan. But to enact it, it was very important that she have some use of her feet. Tied together she did. Tied to the legs of the chair, she'd have been virtually immobile.

Her opportunity would come. She just had to be ready when it did.

RAFE PULLED INTO Heelie at exactly 4:17 p.m. The town of 973 occupants was south and west of Ravesville, but still north of Springfield, Missouri. The terrain was hillier and the roads wound through the limestone cliffs.

While he'd never been to Heelie or Heelie Lake, he suspected it was like many places in the Ozarks, in that the population swelled during the summer when people from all over the country hitched up their boats and drove to Missouri for whatever their particular water sport might be. Fishing. Boating. Waterskiing. Tubing. Canoeing or kayaking for those who wanted to work a little harder.

Based on what he'd seen driving in, Heelie Lake was substantially less commercial than Lake of the Ozarks to the north. Much smaller, too. But that still meant that there were hundreds of miles of shoreline and way too many properties to search efficiently.

He needed help. Which was why he started in town. Bray and Summer had heard from Trish this morning. That meant that she'd been okay at that point. Just maybe, she'd gone to town for one of those lattes that she loved and somebody had seen her.

He started at one end of the business district. At each store, he asked about a woman with long red hair and a German shepherd dog. Finally, in one tattoo parlor, he found a young girl who had seen them.

"I saw her walking by the store earlier," the young woman said. "I noticed her hair right away. It was beautiful. She didn't come in but her dog did stop for a drink." She pointed to the bowl by the door.

"What time?" Rafe asked. It was the first solid clue.

She shrugged. "At least a couple of hours ago," she said. "She was carrying some sacks. I think she'd been to the grocery store."

Then she'd probably been on her way home before the groceries got warm. Which meant that she was probably staying somewhere close. "Her friend Mary Ann Fikus, everybody calls her M.A., was here just a few weeks ago. I think she's staying at the same place. You didn't happen to meet M.A. while she was here?"

She shook her head.

It had been a long shot. He hadn't seen any tattoos on M.A.

"You might want to talk to Bernie Wilberts. He owns a stretch of property on Heelie Lake and his cottages are real nice. She looked like the kind of woman who would enjoy a nice place."

I'm not sleeping on the ground. That was what she'd told him the one time he'd suggested they go camping. He assured her that was no problem. He didn't plan on sleeping and she could be on top.

That had got him a quick shot in the shoulder. Probably because her mother and sister were in the next room. "Where does Bernie live?"

"Molson Road," she said, pointing west. "About a mile from town. Turn right. First house on your left."

Easy enough. "Thank you," he said. His car was parked close, and within seconds, he had the air-conditioning on high and was driving. He found the house in less than five minutes. Nice yard. Long lane with orange daylilies on both sides. Two story, sided yellow. No cars outside.

He got out, knocked on the door and waited. When there was no answer, he tried the front door. It was locked. He walked around the house, looking in the windows. Knocked on the back door. Tried the handle. When there was no answer, he busted a windowpane, stuck his hand in, flipped the lock and entered.

The smell of blood hit him. He pulled his gun and rounded the corner. There, in the narrow hallway between the kitchen and the living room, was a dead person.

A woman. So not Bernie Wilberts. He didn't need a body temperature to know that she'd been dead for several hours. She was already getting stiff.

Three gunshots to the back. A junior detective would be able to figure out that the person who'd killed M.A. had probably also killed this person.

He took a look at her face. Then studied the wedding picture that was on the shelf, next to the flat-screen television. The picture was twenty years old but he was pretty confident that the dead woman was Mrs. Wilberts.

Milo had been knifed to death but M.A. and this woman had both been killed the same way. They were all connected. He knew it.

And it made it seem very likely that the cabins that M.A. had recommended had indeed been owned by Bernie Wilberts.

He looked around for a desk but didn't see one. He started opening drawers and cupboards in the kitchen. In the fourth drawer, he found a stack of paid bills. He quickly went through them, stopping when he came to property tax bills for the previous years. There were eight separate addresses. He entered all of them into the GPS on his phone. Then he put the paperwork back, wiped off everything that he'd touched and left the house.

He would call it in. Just not quite yet. If the killers were close, he didn't want them to get nervous if they heard that their latest victim had been found. They might act rashly and that was the last thing he wanted. He looked at his watch. He still had at least five hours before they would worry about him being back in the States.

He was banking on the fact that they'd keep Trish alive to lure him in. He had no illusions that they'd let her go. Even once they had him. She was as good as dead if he didn't figure out a way to save her.

He studied the map on his phone. All the addresses appeared to be lakeside properties but, unfortunately, not all in the same area. Several were just miles apart but three of them were on the far side of the lake. It would take valuable minutes to drive the distance.

He considered the possibilities. He wanted to be able to approach without detection. With a car, even one that ran as smoothly as the one he was driving, that was impossible. And these were likely not well-traveled roads. A car on them would be noticed. By anybody who was in the mood to notice.

And while he wasn't expected for hours yet, he wasn't going to underestimate his enemy.

It was a sunny, warm day. There were lots of boats on the water. That would be the better way.

He used his smartphone to search for boat rentals. Found the nearest one and drove the seven miles. When he pulled up, there was a man and his little boy already there, renting a fishing boat.

The little guy had red hair.

And for just a minute, he allowed himself to wonder if, had things had gone differently, he and Trish would have had a son. With red hair and big blue eyes.

Trish had wanted a child. Once she'd finally made the decision to get married, she'd jumped in with both feet. Three months after the honeymoon, she'd stopped taking her birth control pills.

When he'd had to leave, he sweated out the first couple of months, until he was sure that he hadn't left her pregnant. He still wouldn't have been able to go back, but he'd have figured out some way to ensure that his child was well taken care of. Just like he'd figured out ways to ensure that Trish was safe, protected.

He'd done a good job.

But now something had gone wrong and Trish was paying the price.

Chapter Eight

Rafe walked inside the boat rental office.

He smiled at the kid behind the counter, who couldn't have been more than twenty. "Got any boats available to rent?"

"Storm's coming in. Not a great time to be on the lake."

"I'll be okay," Rafe said. He pulled out his billfold.

The kid pointed to a sign on the wall. "We rent them in four- or eight-hour increments. But we close at eight. You'll need to have it back by then."

"No problem."

The kid shrugged. "You won't get your full four hours in."

"I'm okay with that," Rafe said easily. He just wanted the kid to get the damn paperwork done so that he could get the hell out of there.

"It's four hundred and a deposit of half that. Bring it back in good shape and you'll get the deposit back."

"Fair enough," Rafe said, pulling out cash.

The kid slid a paper form across the counter. Rafe didn't bother to read the legalese. He filled in his name and showed the kid an ID when he asked for it.

There were coolers on the shelf behind the clerk. "I'll

take one of those, too, with a twelve-pack of water and..."
He grabbed a handful of candy bars from the stand next
to the counter. "And these." Trish was likely to be dehydrated and hungry and... He had to push the next
thoughts out of his head. He'd rescued women before.
Women who'd been kidnapped by men. Women who'd
been used. Badly.

He would kill the men painfully but that would never
be enough to make Trish whole again.

He drew in a deep breath. Focus. He needed to focus.
He handed the kid another fifty to cover the cooler and
the snacks and got seven dollars back.

He didn't pick up the change. Instead, he pointed to a
green hat with netting that covered the neck. "That, too,"
he said, fishing out a few more dollars.

The kid handed it to him. Rafe ripped the tag off and
put it on. It was perfect, with its wide brim.

"I'll meet you around back," the kid said. "*Flora* has
a full tank of gas."

Flora was Trish's mother's name. He hoped that was
a good omen.

He walked back to his car, started it and drove it around
to the rear of the parking lot. He'd flown with guns and
ammunition in his bag and he intended to take them with
him on the boat. He considered taking his second cell
phone but decided not to risk that it could be confiscated
if something went terribly wrong. It would be better left
in the trunk.

He got out of the car, grabbed his duffel and strolled
down the deck. He quickly inspected the boat. *Flora* was
a sturdy-looking twenty-six-footer. He climbed in and
saw that the kid already had loaded the cooler.

"There's your life vest," said the kid. "You're supposed to wear it."

If it wasn't Kevlar, it wasn't going to do him much good. Rafe put it on, then started the boat. Engine seemed solid enough. He waved at the kid and drove away from the dock. He scanned the shoreline, got his bearings. The lake was good sized, at least five, maybe more, miles across. The houses on the far side were barely visible. He would start with those and work his way back. He pulled out his cell phone and used it to identify his first stop.

He took off the clumsy life jacket and ran the boat at a moderate speed, not too slow, not too fast. Because it was a Saturday, there were lots of other boats on the water. When they passed, it wasn't unusual for someone to raise a hand in a friendly wave.

He waved back, making sure that his face was down, as if he was busy with his controls. Even with the hat, no sense letting anybody get too close a look.

When he got to the first property, he docked his boat and walked quietly up to the house that sat very close to the water. He'd always had superior hearing and now he was listening for anything that would tell him that his presence had been detected. But he heard nothing. He got all the way up to the cottage and looked in the window.

It was empty.

But people were living there. There was a pitcher of what appeared to be lemonade on the counter next to an open pack of store-bought cookies. Then he heard the voices. One low. A man. One higher. Probably a woman. But not Trish.

The woman was telling the man to hurry up, that she didn't have all day.

Not exactly sure what he'd see when he edged around

the corner, he almost smiled when he saw the man and woman, both looking as if seventy was a distant memory, playing a board game on the front porch.

He figured it was a safe bet to assume that Trish wasn't inside. He quickly walked back to his boat, got in and motored down to the next cottage.

It was similar to the first but not occupied. It didn't look as if it had been occupied for some time. There were cobwebs stretching across the front door.

He glanced at his watch. He'd already been in Heelie for over an hour. It was almost 5:30. Time was going too fast.

The third and fourth properties were several miles to the south but the GPS showed them very close together. When he got there, he saw that they were larger cottages located across the road from one another. He stood in the woods and surveyed both. There were young boys on bikes in front of one. The other had a teenage girl in a swimsuit sunbathing outside.

Four down, four to go. He got back in his boat and set off for the next location. He had to cross the lake.

He found it easily enough with his GPS but he didn't like the looks of it. It had a longer dock than the other cottages. There was a fifteen-foot aluminum fishing boat tied at the end.

It would be a long walk up that dock. He'd be a sitting duck if somebody in the cottage wanted him dead.

He passed by the dock and drove along the shoreline, as if he might be assessing the best possible place to drop a fishing line. He saw a place that had possibilities. Not for fishing. But for mooring the boat. He'd get his shoes and pants wet but he could live with that. He took off his hat. He didn't want anything to obscure his vision.

He dropped his anchor and waded to shore. Then he scrambled up the bank. He stayed in the tree line all the way back to his destination.

The back of the cottage was all porch, with windows and a door. In order to see in, he'd have to climb the five steps, but that wouldn't do him any good because the blinds were all down. He edged around to the front of the cottage.

Holy hell—there it was. Trish's Jeep.

But no other vehicles. That didn't make sense. Unless they'd come in the fishing boat. He supposed that was possible.

He pulled out his cell phone and studied the picture that he'd been sent. Now, no longer focused on the blood on her face and the gun pressed into her temple, he took in the details and then studied the cottage. She was sitting on a kitchen chair. There was a table and part of a window. He walked around the cottage. The ground sloped off on that side of the cottage, so the window was too high for him to easily see into. But the shape was the same.

The photo had been taken inside of this cottage. It didn't make sense that they'd move her.

Which meant that she was still here.

He considered his options. He had no way of knowing exactly who was inside or how many. But it was always better to divide and conquer.

Trish's Jeep had a car alarm. She'd bought the vehicle two years before and he'd had Milo convince her to get the additional security installed. Now it was going to come in handy.

He walked up to the Jeep and tried the door. As he'd hoped, the alarm started peeping. He was already moving fast, back toward the trees, up at a forty-five-degree angle to the front door.

A man stumbled out of the cottage, looking half-awake. He had a gun in his hand. In the other he must have had a key fob because he raised his arm in the direction of the Jeep and suddenly the alarm stopped.

It made it seem very quiet.

Rafe recognized him. Anthony Paradini. Only son of the New Jersey Paradini clan. His father was Big Tony, who had run the Jersey operation for at least twenty years.

Seeing him made it all the more likely that he'd been right all along. The Maladucci and the Paradini families had been associated for decades. They had competed and collaborated, depending on what particular vice was at play. Big Tony had done fifteen in federal prison for drug trafficking in his twenties and had come out with a bad attitude. Anthony would have been just a little kid when his dad got sent up.

If the Maladucci family needed assistance with something, they would call upon the Paradini family. It would cost them dearly. Nobody worked free of charge.

The price on his head must be pretty high. But even when you paid well, good labor was hard to find.

Anthony was generally considered to be a screwup. Maybe because his dad hadn't been around. Rafe was certain the family wouldn't have trusted him to do this alone. Big Tony was probably inside. Maybe someone else. Maybe not.

Now Anthony was stalking toward the vehicle, to figure out why in hell the alarm had suddenly started ringing. He walked all around the Jeep. Then he looked around.

Rafe picked up a rock and threw it thirty yards. It hit a tree, making noise. As he'd hoped, Anthony focused on the area where the rock had landed. The man raised his gun and started walking toward it.

Oldest trick in the book.

Rafe let him get ten yards into the trees before he took him down with a sharp knock on the back of the head.

He hit him hard. Hard enough to knock him out.

Rafe grabbed the man and dragged him a few feet farther into the woods. One down. But Anthony had been the easy one. Big Tony was a hell of a lot sharper.

Another five minutes and Big Tony would start to wonder where his son had wandered off to. But Rafe doubted that he'd simply barge outside. Big Tony hadn't stayed alive by being careless.

With that in mind, Rafe rolled Anthony onto his back and started unbuttoning his blue-and-white-striped shirt. He got it off, then used the duct tape in his pocket to bind Anthony's wrists together and his ankles, too. Then Rafe slapped a piece of tape over Anthony's mouth.

He left him in the woods, propped up against the tree.

Rafe put on Anthony's shirt. It was tight in the shoulders but would do the trick. Then he took the man's baseball cap and stuck in on his own head.

He stayed back in the trees but worked his way around to the back of the cottage and the lake. There was some yard between the back stairs and the edge of the water. The dock extended another fifty feet.

As quickly as he could, he walked down the dock, listening carefully for any sound from the cottage. A door opening. A window. Anything that would tell him that his presence had been detected.

He was six inches taller than Anthony and twenty pounds heavier, so there was little chance of fooling Big Tony if the man got a close look.

But Rafe got to the end of the dock without hearing anything. Then he sat down, dangled his legs over the edge of the dock and turned his back to the cottage.

To Big Tony's gun.

While Big Tony hadn't stayed alive by being stupid, Rafe Roper hadn't stayed alive by always playing it safe.

Chapter Nine

Old Guy was in the bathroom when the car alarm went off. From behind the closed door, he bellowed for Anthony to go take a look.

A minute later, Anthony stumbled out of the bedroom, swearing loudly. There was a stain on his pants that hadn't been there before and she caught a whiff of alcohol. She suspected Anthony had fallen asleep and spilled the wine on himself.

Her best hope was that he'd come back in, resume drinking and pass out. Then she'd have only the Old Guy to deal with.

"Maybe it's your damn dog," he snarled. He held up the gun in his hand. "I'll finish off the job this time."

Duke. She could feel her throat start to close up and she forced herself to breathe, to not give in to the panic that threatened to overwhelm her. She—

"Anthony!" Old Guy yelled from the bathroom.

Yes, go Anthony, she thought. With him outside and Old Guy indisposed, it was her chance. She had a plan. All she had to do was get to the boat key, grab it with her mouth, then hop, chair and all, to the back door. She thought there was a good possibility that she could turn the knob with her fingers. Once she was outside, all she had to do was hop down the steps, then the length of the dock, throw herself over the edge of the boat, figure out a way to insert the key to start the engine and gun it.

Nothing to it.

Maybe not a foolproof plan but infinitely better than sitting here, waiting for Anthony to snap or Old Guy to get bored and shoot her.

Anthony grabbed her keys off the bookshelf where he'd thrown them earlier. The minute the door shut behind him, she was moving. It wasn't possible to do it quietly, so she simply needed to do it quickly.

Three hops and she was at the counter. She bent forward, snatched the key with her teeth and straightened up. The car alarm had stopped.

Four more hops and she was in the doorway between the main cottage and the porch. Four more and she was at the back door. She turned her body, grabbed the doorknob with the fingers on her left hand and twisted.

She heard it catch at exactly the same minute Old Guy, his pants still unzipped, roared through the archway. His big hand came down on her shoulder and he spun her around so hard that the legs of her chair knocked into the wall, sending her flying.

She and her chair landed sideways on the floor, her right shoulder taking the brunt of the fall. He stood over her. Panting.

"You little bitch," he said. "You'll pay for this." He kicked her hard in the right calf.

She pressed her lips together, determined not to cry out, not to give him the pleasure of knowing that he'd hurt her.

"Anthony," he yelled. He stalked to the front door, leaving her on the floor. She was no threat to him in this position. She couldn't get herself and the chair upright without help. It was like being a crab trying to climb out of a bucket.

It was so frustrating. The only consolation was that he was back within a minute, looking pretty darn frustrated himself.

He yanked her and the chair up and pushed her back into the kitchen. Once all four legs of the chair were back on the ground, he leaned close. He cut the twine that bound her ankles together. Then he quickly tied each ankle to a chair leg.

"I swear to all that's holy," he muttered, "between you and that kid, a man can't even have a moment of peace to do his business in the bathroom."

She didn't intend to give these two any peace. This was a momentary setback but she wasn't giving up.

"What do you want from me?" she asked.

He stared at her. "I don't want anything from you," he said finally. "You're simply a means to an end."

"What end?"

He smiled and pinched her bruised cheek hard. "Justice, sweetheart. Long overdue, from what I understand."

Then he walked over to the front door one more time and looked out. Shaking his head, he went out to the porch.

She could hear the blind being raised. Then the sound of a door opening. "Anthony, get your ass back inside this cottage," Old Guy yelled.

"ANTHONY, GET YOUR ass back inside this cottage."

He'd been right. It was Big Tony.

Rafe kept sitting.

He heard footsteps on the stairs. Then nothing. He assumed Big Tony was crossing the yard.

So far, so good.

Then heavy footsteps on the dock, making it shake just a little. "This ain't a damn fishing trip," Big Tony said, agitation clear.

Rafe didn't move.

Now the footsteps came faster. "I'm talking to you, boy."

Rafe judged him to be about five feet away. He pulled his legs up, got them under him and sprang up and around, all in one motion.

Big Tony was close enough that Rafe's first punch landed squarely on the man's haggard cheek.

To Big Tony's credit, he responded faster than Anthony ever would have, getting in one good punch, knocking Rafe's head back. But Rafe was faster, more agile, and in less than thirty seconds, the fight was over.

Big Tony was flat on his stomach, his arm twisted behind him, breathing heavily. Rafe, with one knee in the middle of Tony's back, leaned close to the older man's ear.

"I'm going to let you live. For the moment. But if we get inside and I see that you've harmed one hair on her head, I'm going to kill you. And it will be an extremely painful death."

Big Tony didn't answer.

And Rafe found himself hesitating. He had been full steam ahead when it had been about getting here and making sure that Trish was safe. But now? Now that he was about to give the woman that he'd loved the surprise of her lifetime, he was scared.

He'd never wanted to hurt her. Had never wanted to cause her pain. And he'd done exactly that.

But he'd kept her alive.

That was what was important.

All the while keeping an eye on the cottage, he slapped a piece of duct tape over Big Tony's mouth, then secured his wrists and ankles. He left him lying facedown on the dock. If the idiot was stupid enough to roll around and fall into the water and drown, that wasn't his concern.

He took off Anthony's striped shirt and baseball hat. Then he drew in a breath, steadied his nerves and continued up to the house.

He was fairly confident that it was only Anthony and Big Tony in the cottage but he wasn't going to be stupid about it. He opened the back door and edged his head around the frame. The porch was empty. He listened, didn't hear anything.

But he knew Trish was close. Could feel her presence.

He crossed the porch and stepped into the main room of the cottage. There, tied to a chair, was his one true love.

She stared at him, her pretty green eyes registering shock. She opened her mouth, as if to speak, then closed it.

"Trish," he said.

Her eyes rolled back in her head and she fainted.

He took one extra second to clear the bedroom and bath, making sure that there was nobody else in the small cottage. Then he took his knife and sliced through the twine that bound her wrists and her ankles. The coarse material had worn against her delicate skin, and his hands, his always-steady hands, shook as he balled up the twine and tossed it aside.

Just as she was coming to, he saw the bruise on her

cheek. He reached out to touch it but dropped his hand. He didn't want to see her go lights-out again.

If he'd expected her to throw her arms around him and swear to love him forever, he would have been sadly mistaken. Instead, she pushed her chair back, away from him. When there was space, she got up, on unsteady legs, and backed away from him until she came up against the wall that separated the bath from the kitchen.

She still hadn't said a word. It rattled him.

"Did they touch you?" he asked. He knew immediately it was the wrong thing to say first but he couldn't help it. She looked so vulnerable and he couldn't stand that she'd been terrorized by Big Tony and his idiot son.

She did not respond for a long moment. Then finally, she shook her head. "I thought...you were dead," she said, her voice barely a whisper.

And a dozen lies popped into his head. He could pretend that he'd been badly injured and just recovered his memory. He could say that he'd been taken prisoner. He could...

He was tired of the lies. So tired. "I know," he said.

"You bastard," she said, her voice rising sharply.

Mindful of the two men that he had tied up outside, he didn't defend himself. "Where's Duke?" he asked, looking around.

Now her eyes were big. "How do you know my dog's name?"

He wasn't doing well here. But he knew something was wrong if Duke wasn't close. She hadn't left him in Ravesville. "I'll explain. Where is he?"

"Anthony shot him," she said.

Rafe clamped down on the rage that arched through

him. He was well aware of how much Trish loved that dog. "I'm sorry," he said.

"I think he's dead," she said. "He managed to get away into the woods."

He couldn't worry about it right now but he would find the dog. He was a fine animal and he certainly deserved better. "Just give me a few minutes to get things right here."

She was shaking. That just about killed him. But there really were things to do.

"Please," he said, before going out the front door. Anthony was still where he'd left him. The man was conscious but definitely not firing on all cylinders. Rafe put his gun in the man's face and waited until it registered. Then he pulled the man to his feet. And punched him in the mouth. Hard. The man went to his knees. Rafe yanked him up again. "That was for the dog," he said.

Then he shoved him in the direction of the cottage. Once inside, he tied him to the same kitchen chair where Trish had been restrained.

"Let's see how you like it," Rafe said, wrapping his wrists tight to the back of the chair. Then he went out the porch door to get Big Tony. He brought him inside.

Trish had moved from the wall to the sofa on the porch. "I'll just be a minute," he said to her. He was finishing tying Big Tony to another chair when he heard the back door open and close. He moved fast.

Trish was outside. Halfway down the dock, bent from the waist. He didn't think she was throwing up but maybe she felt faint.

He understood. His own knees were damn weak.

He understood why he'd given almost no thought to what he might say to her when he saw her. There were really no words that were adequate. And what he'd said could certainly have been better. But he would explain. Maybe not everything. But enough that she would understand he'd done the only thing he could do.

He went back to make sure that he'd done a good job with securing both of the Paradinis. He had questions for them but it could wait until he made sure that Trish was okay.

He was putting his knife back in his boot when he heard the sound of an engine turn over, sputter for a minute, then smooth out. He was out the door and down the steps in one leap. Then it was full steam ahead as he saw Trish yank on the tie rope of the fishing boat.

She was leaving.

Over his dead body.

She was behind the wheel. Giving it gas. It had better pickup than he would have anticipated.

He realized he wasn't going to be in time to stop her. Damn it. He ran through the trees and waded out to *Flora*. He pulled up his anchor and took off. Unless her boat ran way faster than it looked, it would be no contest.

Sure enough, in just minutes, he caught up with Trish. Her hair was blowing in the wind and she had both hands on the steering wheel, white-knuckled. She was not wearing a life vest. He recalled that she was not a terribly strong swimmer.

He did not want her to do something stupid and end up in the water. He slowed his own boat down, hoping that she'd do the same. But she didn't let up.

"Slow down," he yelled.

She didn't respond.

He looked around. It was after seven and there would normally be more than an hour of daylight, but the storm was rolling in and it was getting dark. Most of the boats were off the lake. But there could still be people onshore who might get interested if they heard too many shouts coming off the lake.

He gave her some space. He followed, but not so close that anyone would get the impression that he was chasing her. He didn't intend to let her get away, and if she got in any trouble, he wanted to be close enough to quickly help.

"Just don't do anything stupid," he murmured, then realized he wasn't sure if he was talking to her or to himself. Probably to himself, he realized.

Because right now he was feeling pretty damn dumb. How had he thought he could ever really leave this woman? How had he thought he could be content with just observing her life from afar?

He wanted to be a part of her life. To be with her.

But despite all his efforts, all the sacrifices, he'd put her in danger. And if he didn't end it now, it was going to hang over their heads like a guillotine. Just waiting. A sharp blade at the ready.

Chapter Ten

Trish felt as if her head was going to explode. Rafe. Alive.

The events of the past half hour were more than any one person could be expected to take in, to process. It was asking too much. All she could do, it seemed, was drive the boat.

She had no destination in mind. Had already lost track of where she'd started. Not that she had any intention of going back to the cottage. She would make arrangements for her Jeep to be returned to Ravesville. Bray would do it for her. She could ask him to look for Duke, too. It was a long shot to even hope that he'd somehow survived but he certainly deserved to have a decent burial.

Her hands started to shake and she gripped the steering wheel tighter. She'd lost a dog and gained a husband.

Who was following her in his boat.

She'd heard him yell at her to slow down but there had been no way in hell she was doing that. Her emotions were too raw.

She had mourned him for four years. And he'd been living the whole time. It made her feel stupid, as if someone smarter would have figured it out.

She had never, not even once, considered that he might still be alive. Even when his body had never been recovered.

Because what kind of person did something like that? What kind of person would put another human being through the trauma of having a loved one die?

Certainly not the man that she'd married. Or that she thought she'd married.

But maybe she hadn't really known Rafe Roper at all.

If that was even his real name. If everything else was bogus, then maybe his name was, too.

For years now, she'd politely corrected people when they'd called her Trish Wright. *Trish Wright-Roper*, she would say. Well, ha-ha, maybe the joke was on her.

She'd seen him a hundred times in her dreams. And she'd talked to him. On her good days, she'd told him over and over again how much she loved him. On her bad days, she'd railed at him for being careless in the river.

But he'd never answered her, never said anything.

Today, when he'd said her name, his voice sounded rusty. But yet so familiar.

It had been too much.

When he'd been tying up Anthony and Old Guy, she'd felt as if she was about to crawl out of her skin. She'd had to get outside, get some fresh air. As she neared the back door, she saw the boat key that she'd dropped on the floor when Old Guy had stopped her escape attempt. She picked it up, with still no plan in mind.

But she'd had the presence of mind to get her gun from underneath the sofa cushion. She walked outside, hoping to catch her breath. She stood and looked across the lake. Saw the black clouds rolling in. She felt as if they were going to roll right over her and she would be smothered.

And just that quick she decided that she had to leave. She ran for the small fishing boat. And he almost caught her. In fact, she'd been afraid that he was going to leap from the dock into her boat.

She hadn't realized that he had a boat just down the shoreline. But he must have known it would easily catch up to hers, even with her head start.

And now the lake was really getting dark and the wind was picking up. Even with the headlights on, it was getting difficult to see the shore. She looked at her gas tank. It was nearing empty. She did not want to be stranded on the water all night in the middle of a raging storm. That was just stupid.

Would Rafe just keep circling her? Waiting for some indication that she was ready to talk?

It was ironic. A day ago, she'd have said that she'd give anything to have just one more conversation with him, to tell him how much she loved him. But now she didn't know how she was going to do it. But putting it off wasn't going to make it easier.

She throttled down the boat and headed for shore. When she saw an empty boat slip, she cut her speed even further and managed to slide into place, bumping the side of the boat just once against the wooden dock. She grabbed the tie rope and tossed the looped end around one of the wood posts.

She reached for her gun that she'd had on the seat next to her. Then she got out and was standing on the dock, her arms wrapped around herself, when Rafe smoothly docked his own boat on the other side. When he killed his lights, the area was very dark.

There were a few lights still on the water, boaters who were probably hurrying to shore. Bits of light from nearby cottages split the dark woods.

"Hi," he said softly, coming to stand next to her. He

had a flashlight in his hand. He didn't try to touch her. "Are you okay?"

"Not really," she said. She unwrapped her arms and he must have seen her gun because he held up his hands.

"Planning on using that on me?" he asked, his tone casual.

"I had it stuffed under the sofa cushion on the porch," she explained, choosing not to answer his question.

"I'm glad you've got it," he said. "And I'm sorry," he added. "I'm sorry I surprised you and that I did a horrible job of explaining what was going on."

"What is going on, Rafe?" she asked. "If that is your name."

"My name is Rafe Roper," he said, his voice tight.

She'd offended him. Well, tough. "Well, then, maybe you want to explain why everything I've believed for the last four years has been a lie? A deliberate lie."

"I—"

"And how the hell did you know I was here?" she asked, interrupting him.

He waited, maybe to see if another question was coming. Maybe because he was thinking of a good lie. She had no idea. She didn't know him.

"Well?" she said, her tone impatient.

"I learned of Milo's death and I anticipated that you might be vulnerable."

"Milo," she repeated. "You…" Her voice trailed off. "You didn't even know Milo. What difference would his death have made to you?"

"I knew Milo," he said.

"You were already…dead," she said, her voice breaking.

"I was gone," he said. "Not dead. Milo and I had

worked together for years. He was in Ravesville because I arranged for him to be there."

"He had been in prison," she said.

"No. Never. That was a story that was invented for him."

He was dismantling everything she'd believed to be true. Her chest felt tight. The air heavy. It was hard to breathe. "You arranged for Milo to be there. To do what? To spy on me?"

"To look after you. I was attempting to manage a difficult situation."

"Manage a difficult situation," she again repeated his words, her tone flat. "That's great. Just great," she emphasized, more agitated. "I was mourning a dead husband and you were *managing me*."

He didn't answer. She was so angry that it was taking everything she had not to push him off the dock into the water.

"I'll tell you everything," he said. "But I need to deal with those two back at the cottage first. We can't risk them getting loose or someone coming to assist them."

The idea of having to deal with Old Guy and Anthony again was chilling.

"Will you come with me in my boat?" he asked.

He was stiff and formal, acting as if one wrong word on his part would send her running off into the woods. It almost made her feel bad.

If she didn't go with him, she would have to stay here, by herself, in the dark. Plus, her Jeep was back at the cottage. She could get it and drive herself home. She would find Duke's body and she would drive both of them home. "Yes," she said. She would pay someone to come get Bernie Wilberts's boat and return it to the cottage.

He held out his hand to help her into the boat but she ignored it. She wasn't ready yet to touch him. He didn't force the issue. He waited until she was in, then stepped over the edge, untied the line and started the engine.

She had no idea where they needed to go but he didn't seem worried. He aimed the front of the boat toward the far-off shore. He sat behind the wheel. She sat in the back, as far away from him as she could get.

BERNIE WILBERTS HAD a buzz going that wasn't helping him as he navigated the winding roads. He'd left his house more than fourteen hours ago, shortly after having a silent breakfast with his wife. There had been a time when he and Amy had talked, laughed, loved. But lately, because of the situation, conversation between the two of them was forced.

She didn't understand that this was the only way to protect the family. He hadn't worked his whole life to provide for his three daughters and his wife only to have it go up in smoke because of a few mistakes. His youngest was still in college. And his middle daughter was getting married in the fall. All of that cost money.

He'd found a way to atone for his screwup at work that had cost him his job. He'd replaced his income. His wife should be congratulating him, not busting his chops. She was still able to stay home and do enough online shopping to keep the UPS driver busy. She wasn't complaining about that. Nope.

Everybody in this part of the country made a living off drugs—in some form or fashion. It wasn't that big of a deal. Who cared if a few idiots overdosed and died? They were losers.

Not like his girls. All three of them had been on homecoming court. Beautiful, they were.

Like that woman, Trish. She was something with all that red hair, down to her waist. And really sweet, too.

The idea that something bad was going to happen to her in the next day or two had settled on his chest and he hadn't slept well. Which was why, after breakfast, he'd packed up his fishing gear and gone out onto the lake. He'd stayed out past dinnertime and it was dark by the time he'd got back to shore, grabbed a bite at the Hoot and Shoot Diner. The storm was about to break.

He felt sick. The twelve-pack on the boat and then the two whiskeys straight up at the diner probably contributed to that.

Indecision and alcohol didn't mix.

He'd weighed his options. Do nothing. That was the easiest, probably the best for everyone. Well, not for pretty Trish. Or he could stop at the cottage and tell her to go home. Not tell her why but simply tell her to get the hell home and not tell anybody that he'd warned her.

Could he trust her to keep her mouth shut? Even if she did, would DT take it out on him that she'd disappeared? If she told the truth, it was a foregone conclusion that DT would enact his revenge.

Getting mixed up with that man had been his big mistake. But what choice had he had? He'd had some bad luck with cards. And then hadn't been able to pay back the loans. That was when DT had come into the picture. DT had told him that he could either treat the offer to join his operation and regain financial stability as the gift it was or if he refused, DT would make him regret his lack of manners. And then DT had laughed and asked if he'd got his mail yet that day.

He had. It had been a picture of Amy and his daughters having lunch at a local restaurant.

So, he'd gone along. And the money had been good. The local kids were hungry for their heroin and Amy was happy because he told her their investments were doing well. Then one day, he hadn't been careful enough and Amy had found his inventory. It had been right about the same time that a couple of his customers overdosed and died.

Amy was a teacher and she'd had the kids in her fourth-grade class just six years earlier. She acted as if he was some kind of monster. He hadn't been able to tell her the truth. If she'd known that their girls were at risk, she'd have never forgiven him. He told her he had it under control. She said he'd crossed a line that he could never step back over.

Now what would she think of what he was doing with Trish? He hadn't even understood the plan at first. All he'd been told was to keep the cottage available. Then he'd been told that M.A. Fikus would be renting it. She'd stayed a few days, but when he'd stopped in to see her, she'd been cold to the point of rudeness. He'd dismissed it until DT had mentioned that M.A. Fikus would be referring the cottage to Trish Wright-Roper and that he should cut the rate by half.

He'd been irritated about the reduced rent, but since DT was paying him well for other things, he'd kept his mouth shut. But he had said he was surprised that M.A. Fikus was referring anyone, since she hadn't seemed happy while she was here.

DT had laughed and said that if she wanted to keep her employer from learning that she had a nasty little heroin habit, she'd do what she was supposed to do.

He hadn't asked DT why it was so important to get Trish Wright-Roper to the cottage. He didn't want to know.

But once he'd seen her, he suspected the worst. Stories about young women captured and hidden away for years to be used by the men holding them had kept him up most of the night. Was that her future? He'd always suspected DT was a little bent.

She probably wasn't all that much older than his oldest daughter, whom he'd taken, along with her sons—his only grandchildren—out onto the lake just two weeks ago.

He didn't think Trish had any children but still.

His decision made, he cranked the wheel sharply and headed for the cottage. He'd warn her. What she chose to do with that warning was her business. He parked his car next to Trish's Jeep. There were no lights on in the cottage, which meant that she might be sleeping. But better to lose a few hours of sleep than...

He didn't even want to think it.

He rested his forehead against the steering wheel. He'd made a damn mess out of his life. Got himself in a hole that he couldn't climb out of.

Disappointed Amy. That was for sure. And she'd been a good wife. Most of the time.

He didn't think they could go back to where they'd been, but maybe this was one step in the right direction. Maybe saving Trish would make the difference. He pulled out his cell phone and sent a text to his wife. I'll be home soon. Stopping at one of the rental cottages.

He got out of the car. She hadn't turned on the outside lights and it was very dark. If he hadn't known the area so well, he might have fallen.

He knocked.

No one answered.

Not knowing what else to do, he entered the combination and opened the door. The room smelled bad.

His stomach rolling with whiskey and grease, he hit the light. Two men were tied to chairs. He did not know them.

They both had duct tape on their mouths. He ripped the tape off the younger one's mouth.

"Thank God," he said.

Bernie stared at him. "Who are you?" he asked.

"Anthony," the man said.

That meant nothing to Bernie. "Who's that?" he asked, pointing to the older man.

"My father. Untie us."

Bernie shook his head. Where was Trish? What had happened here? He walked over to the older man and ripped the tape off his mouth.

"What the hell are you doing here?" the man asked.

Bernie recognized the voice. It was him. DT. That was what Bernie had dubbed him because he was always telling him what to do. Do this. Do that. DT.

"Don't just stand there like a dumbass," DT said, in the same demanding tone that Bernie had grown to hate more each day.

"Where's the woman?" Bernie asked.

"Not far enough," DT said. "And when I find her and her husband, they will both be very sorry."

So she was married. "Maybe you should just cut your losses and call it a day," Bernie said.

DT stared at him, his eyes hostile. It reminded him of how angry the man had been when Bernie had told him that Amy had discovered what was going on. DT had become so angry on the telephone, had said he wouldn't tolerate any more careless mistakes.

He was probably outliving his usefulness to DT. Maybe this was the way it was all supposed to end. His ultimate penance for crimes committed. Odd, but that gave him the sense of the peace he'd been searching for the whole damn day on the lake.

But what about Amy?

He opened the kitchen drawer to find a knife.

Chapter Eleven

Trish sat as still as a statue for most of the ride. But once they had got across the lake and close to shore, she made her way up to the front of the boat. "What are you going to do with them?" she asked.

"Trust me on this," he said, then winced when he realized how inappropriate the words were. "They'll pay for what they did to you, to Milo, to Duke, to the others," he finished.

"The others?" she said, her eyes wide.

There was really no good way to tell her. "M.A. Fikus is dead."

"What?" She paused. "I don't understand," she added.

Her voice sounded weaker and he was afraid that she was going to faint again. He reached for her, but when she flinched and drew back, he dropped his hand. "Please, sit," he said. He relaxed when she did, lowering herself awkwardly into the passenger seat.

"You found out about the cottage from M.A., right?"

"Yes."

"I don't think that was an accident. She told you about the cottage for a reason."

"M.A. was my friend," she said, shaking her head.

He understood. She was questioning whether it was

another betrayal. "Maybe she didn't have bad intent. Unfortunately, we may never know. Or perhaps one of the two inside will fill in the missing blanks if they think it will help them in some way."

"With the police?" she asked.

He ratcheted back the throttle as they got closer to shore. Big Tony and Anthony wouldn't be as concerned about the police as they would be their boss, once it became known that they had failed. But he didn't have time to explain all that right now. He wanted a chance to question them and then he would call his team, call his boss. "Yes, the authorities will be notified."

She closed her eyes. "And then what happens."

Then he was going to finish this. Once and for all. "I stash you somewhere safe, under twenty-four-hour guard."

"I'm going home," she said. "Back to Ravesville."

"We can discuss that," he said carefully.

She held up a hand. "Do. Not. Try. To. *Manage*. Me." She spit out each word. "I think you've done enough of that." She turned, so that her back was facing him. Her spine was straight. Brittle.

It dawned on him that maybe she hated him. That thought made him want to vomit over the side of the boat.

This was not going to be easy.

He focused intently upon the shore. He needed to deal with one thing at a time.

The sky was heavy with swirling clouds. When he cut his lights three hundred yards out, it was as if they were moving in a sea of blackness. He slowed way down and used his flashlight to find his way to the dock. He killed the engine. "I want you to stay in the boat," he said quietly. "Please," he added, realizing she wasn't inclined to do anything he suggested. "If you have any reason to think anything is wrong, then get the hell out of here. Don't worry about me."

"Don't you think you're taking a big risk that I'll simply leave you here?" she asked.

She'd left him once already tonight. But she'd had a chance to calm down. Had learned some things that might give her pause before she ran off in the dark night. "I guess I'll have to take my chances."

He tied up and turned to her. He kept his hand over his flashlight, mostly obscuring the light. But he could see her shape. "Get down," he said, "on the floor. There's less chance of anyone seeing you. Keep your gun in your hand. If anybody besides me approaches the boat, shoot them. Don't make small talk first. Just shoot them."

He waited until she got down on the floor of the boat. Only then did he turn and step up on the dock. He listened carefully for any sound that told him his presence had been detected.

He didn't hear anything.

Then he did. And saw a familiar arc in the night sky.

But it still caught him off guard when he was knocked back by a fiery blast.

THE BLAST SHOOK the dock and the boat. And then a heavy splash sent the water rippling.

And the stench of burning wood filled the air.

Trish felt as if she couldn't catch her breath. The cottage had blown up and was now burning. And Rafe— *oh my God*—Rafe had been blown off the dock, into the lake.

She had to find him. The fire lit up the space and she saw his body. Facedown, five feet from the dock.

She threw herself over the edge of the boat and slogged through the chest-high water. When she reached him, she yanked hard on his right shoulder, to flip him over.

He wasn't breathing.

Cognizant that there must be danger nearby, she didn't yell or scream. But she shook him.

No response.

She grabbed him under his arms and towed him back to the dock. Even with the buoyancy of water, he was very heavy. Panting hard, she braced herself against the ladder at the end of the dock. She had his back against her front. With her knee bent and under his lower back, it gave her enough leverage to keep his head out of the water.

"Damn you," she cried, her mouth close to his ear. "Don't you die on me now." She wrapped her arms around him and squeezed, the heels of her hands digging into his chest. She did it three times in a row. Hard.

And when he sputtered and spit water, it was the best sound she'd ever heard. Then he was twisting in her arms.

He was running his hands over her arms, holding her face. "Are you injured?" he demanded.

"No. You are. You almost drowned," she said.

He ignored her. "We have to get back in the boat. We have to get out of here."

And with more strength than she would have anticipated, he was pushing her up and over the side of the boat. Then crawling in himself. Before pulling away, he leaned over the side and grabbed his flashlight off the dock, dropping it in her lap.

She turned it on and pointed it at him.

There was blood running down the side of his face from a substantial gash in his forehead, near the hairline.

She suspected he'd hit his head on the dock before he'd gone into the water.

"You're bleeding," she said. "You need a doctor."

He reached up to feel his head. "It's fine," he said. "Hang on." He started the boat.

"What happened here?" she demanded.

"Rocket launcher," he said as if that was all she needed to know. He took the flashlight from her hand and focused it forward.

As they drove away, she turned her head to look at the remains of the cottage. She had never seen anything like it. It was all just too much. The men holding her prisoner. Rafe. Learning that everything she'd believed to be true for four years had been a lie. Now this.

Rafe had not yet turned on the lights, and as they edged away from shore, the light from the fire diminished. She forced herself to stand and move to the front of the boat. "Hold this," he said, handing her the flashlight.

He reached into his wet jeans and pulled out a cell phone. She expected him to try to turn it on, to see if it had survived the lake. But, instead, he removed the battery.

"What are you doing?" she asked.

"We're going off the grid," he said.

She waited for something more, but when it didn't seem to be coming, she grabbed his arm. "What the hell are you talking about?" she said. "We have to call someone. Get help."

He shook his head. "Ain't no helping anybody who was inside. They're dead."

He was undoubtedly right and that sat heavy in her stomach. A chill spread through her. Some of that, she realized, was that she was in wet clothes, speeding along in a boat. But mostly she was cold to the bone because had the explosion happened an hour earlier, she'd have been inside. She'd be dead now, too.

"I don't understand any of this," she said.

He turned his head. It was too dark to see his eyes but she knew what she would see. Grim determination. She could hear it in his voice. "I don't, either. And until I do, we're staying away from the cottage."

"But—"

He held up a hand. "Listen, Trish. This wasn't an accident. We have to figure out what's going on."

If it hadn't been an accident, then there were really only two choices. "Was it someone going after me or after those men?"

"I don't know. Listen, there are things you don't know."

The part of her that was fed up with surprises wanted to stop him. She couldn't handle anything else. But she said nothing. This was a dangerous situation that didn't appear to be getting any better. She needed to know everything if she had any hope of getting out of this alive.

Alive. Summer. The two thoughts collided in her head at the same moment. She pulled again on Rafe's arm.

"I have to be able to call Summer. My Jeep was at that cottage. It's a simple matter for them to trace it back to me, then to Ravesville. If they contact the local police, that's going to be Chase Hollister. He's going to tell Summer."

"We may not be able to help that."

She grabbed him, hard enough to swing him her direction. "I am not going to have Summer believe that I'm dead. Not for one minute. I know what that does to a person."

She could feel the emotion in his big body. And she felt bad that she'd blurted it out just that way, given that earlier she'd noticed that his voice was filled with pain.

She suspected that he probably had a concussion in addition to the laceration that needed attention. But he needed to understand that this was nonnegotiable.

"We'll find a phone," he said. "As quickly as possible. I promise."

After everything that had happened, it was crazy to think that she could ever trust him. But oddly enough, she believed him.

"But first," he said, "we're going back to where we landed earlier. I saw a cottage set back from the lake about two hundred yards. There were no lights."

"Maybe they were in bed."

"Maybe. But we should at least check it out. It's going to rain, maybe even storm, and I'm not crazy about spending the night on the lake in a boat in those conditions."

"Why are we looking for shelter? We should be going to the police," she said, again trying to make him see reason.

"No," he said.

She knew there was no use arguing. They moved quickly across the lake. As they got closer to shore, he cut the engine back. Now she could hear the very distant noise of sirens. The explosion would likely have been heard for miles. Firefighters were responding. She was very grateful for the recent rain and that the ground and surrounding foliage was wet. Perhaps the fire would not spread too far.

He held a finger up to his lips. She understood. They were near shore and wouldn't want their voices overheard. She would not have been able to identify the right spot were it not for Bernie Wilberts's boat that was still tied on one side of the U-shaped dock.

He docked the boat and tied it up. "Bring your gun," he said. Before he stepped out, he pulled on a fishing hat that had been in the boat. Then he got out and turned to offer her a hand. Instinctively, she took it but knew immediately it was a mistake when her skin, her traitorous flesh, heated up fast.

She had always loved his touch.

Had missed it so.

The minute her feet were on the dock, she dropped her arm, breaking contact. This man had let her think he was dead for four years.

And now he was back, with trouble everywhere.

"This way," he said softly. He also had his gun in his hand. The flashlight in the other.

He led her away from the lake. The grass was long, up to her knees in places. The wind whipped it around them. It did not bode well if the cottage was still burning.

She turned around to look and realized the angle was wrong. She could no longer see the other shore, see the cottage where she'd been so happy and relaxed this morning, only to be held prisoner there later.

The long, wild grass turned into a short, mowed lawn. The cottage was just in front of them. If the grass had been mowed recently, how likely was it that the cottage was empty? But Rafe kept going.

They walked around to the front. There was no garage and no car in the driveway. So far, so good.

"Stay right here," Rafe whispered, pulling her off to the side.

"What are you doing?" she rasped.

"I'm going to knock on the door," he said. "If somebody answers, I'll give them some excuse about trouble with my boat. Just stay out of sight, no matter what."

"I should knock. You'll scare them. You've got blood all over your face."

He pulled his hat lower onto his forehead. "Your hair is…memorable. We can't take the chance."

She watched him walk away. *Memorable*. He used to call her hair sexy. When they would make love, he would run his hands through it. When she would wake up in the mornings, he would often have thick strands of it wrapped around his hand, and she would know that at some point in the middle of the night, he had reached out for her.

It was so dark that even though she was probably less than ten feet away from him, she could not see him. But she heard him knock loudly on the door. Then a second time.

"This way," he said, his voice soft and close to her ear.

She couldn't quite keep her squeal inside. She hadn't heard a thing as he'd walked back to her. How the hell did he do that?

"Sorry," he said, his voice sounding amused for the first time. "I'm going in through the window around back. Then I'll open the back door for you. I'll need you to hold the light for me."

When she shone the flashlight, she realized he had a knife in his hand. In less than a minute, he'd scored a neat square in the glass. He pushed it through with his palm and reached his hand and arm inside, up to the elbow. She heard the sound of a latch flipping.

She moved the light, enough that she could see his face. Sweat was running off it, yet he was shaking. "Rafe," she said. "You need to—"

"Stay here," he interrupted her. Then he raised the window, threw a leg over the side and was out of sight.

It dawned on her that there was a great deal that she didn't know about this man that she'd married.

He opened the back door. "Come in. The place is empty."

Empty, yes, but definitely recently inhabited. With the help of Rafe's flashlight, she could see that there were clean dishes in the rack next to the sink and newspapers on the table. When she got closer, she could see they had last Sunday's date. When she lifted up the paper, she saw an electric bill for Edith and Harry Norton.

She opened the refrigerator. It contained the basics: ketchup, mustard, mayonnaise, jelly. And in the produce compartments, sweet potatoes and onions. Things that wouldn't spoil quickly. There were no milk or eggs. She closed the door.

There wasn't much to see in the rest of the space. Next to the kitchen was a small living room, then a bedroom and a bath. It was very similar to Bernie Wilberts's cottage except that it was smaller, with no back porch.

That didn't matter, she realized. She didn't intend to stay long. Just long enough for the storm to pass and for Rafe to provide her with some explanation of what was going on.

"I think it's likely that the Nortons use this cottage on the weekends," Rafe said.

"This is the weekend," she said. "It's Saturday."

"I know. So I think that's good news. If the people who come here aren't here by Saturday night, they aren't coming this weekend. I think we just got lucky."

He might be right or maybe the people were coming on Sunday this week. There could be a thousand reasons for that. But she didn't deny that it felt good to be off the lake, away from the potential of the upcoming storm. And she was pretty confident that Rafe couldn't go much longer. He was trying to hide it, but she didn't miss that he was leaning against the counter, as if his legs were not quite up to carrying his body weight.

"You need to get that cut cleaned up. Sit down," she said, as she gently pulled him toward one of the kitchen chairs.

She set the flashlight on the counter to give off some light. Then she grabbed paper towels off the roll that hung next to the sink. She ran the kitchen faucet until the water got warm. "Can we turn on the lights?" she asked.

"I'd rather we didn't," he said. "But we can light this," he added, nodding at the large candle that was in the middle of the kitchen table. He picked up the book of matches next to the candle and struck one.

"There's no phone," she said, unable to keep the disappointment from her voice. "We can't call Summer."

"We wouldn't take the chance of doing it from here anyway. It's possible that they've thought ahead far enough that they've got some kind of tracking device on your sister's phone and they'd be able to locate us here."

Who were these people? "Would you have thought to do that?"

He nodded. "Yes. I'd have identified anybody who might be in your support network and made sure that I was monitoring their activity."

And she'd thought she couldn't feel any more helpless. Guess that was another thing she was wrong about.

She pushed the candle closer to him. It wasn't much light but certainly better than nothing.

Using the damp paper towel that she'd had clutched in her hand, she gently wiped away the blood on his face. The cut was several inches long but not too deep. He did have a hell of a knot about an inch above his right eyebrow. "I think you hit the deck before you went into the water. Hard enough that it knocked you out. You probably have a concussion."

"It'll be fine." He dismissed her concern. He gently caught her wrist. "Thank you," he said softly. "I'd have drowned if you hadn't helped me."

She stepped back, suddenly chilled in the overly warm room. "This time for real," she said.

The words hung in the air.

"I'm going to see if there are any first aid supplies in the bathroom," she said, desperately needing to put a few feet between them. He didn't try to stop her.

She shut the door behind her and turned on the light. Her legs were shaking and she lowered herself to the floor in the small bathroom. *This time for real.* It had been a mean thing to say. And that wasn't generally her style. But while she hadn't hit her head, she still felt pretty damn off-balance.

M.A. was dead. The two men in the house as well. And, of course, Milo. Was that where the trail started?

It had somehow led them to this cottage. She knew pure determination had fueled Rafe for the past fifteen minutes. The blast, the knock on the head, the time in the water... It had all taken a toll. But if she hadn't seen it all, she'd have never known.

Rafe Roper was a hell of an actor.

And that was why she was sitting on the floor, pretending to be studying the contents of a bathroom cupboard.

She was afraid. Afraid that she was going to learn that it had all been an act. Maybe that was why she'd snapped first. To get the first swing in so that when the knockout punch came, she'd at least have one small victory to hang on to.

This time for real. Take that, Rafe Roper.

She heard the scrape of a chair and knew that he was just seconds from coming to check on her. She grabbed what she needed and stood so fast that her reflection in the mirror almost seemed blurred.

She looked horrible. Her hair was wet and snarled from her time in the water, her face pale, her eyes dark. But, she realized, if Rafe hadn't freed her from that cottage, she'd look a whole lot worse because she'd be dead.

She turned off the light before she opened the door. Then she walked back to the kitchen and placed the tube of antibiotic ointment on the table. Then the adhesive strips. "I think the butterfly kind would be better to close the cut, but this is all they have."

"It'll be fine," he said.

She placed the last thing on the table, a big bottle of ibuprofen. "I thought this might come in handy," she said.

He smiled. "I think it's good that I've got a hard head."

She stood close to him and liberally spread the ointment on the cut. Then she opened three of the strips and covered it.

"Can I get you anything else?" she asked, rather formally, perhaps, for the circumstances.

"I'm good," he said.

He wasn't but there might not be time to waste. "I want to know something," she said. "Before he died, Milo said to me, 'Tell Rafe they know.' I thought he was delirious. But he wasn't, was he? They? Who is that? Who is doing this? And what is it that they know?"

Chapter Twelve

She wanted answers. Well, she deserved some. But it would likely have been easier going if his head wasn't pounding and he wasn't seeing double.

Although two of Trish was not necessarily a bad thing. She'd saved his life. He was confident of that. All he basically remembered was the heat from the explosion, the force of it knocking him back, falling, pain and then nothing.

Except for that his very last thought had been of her. And a prayer that somehow she had escaped injury and would follow his orders to get the hell out of there.

Instead, she'd gone overboard and dragged his sorry hide out of the water. He'd been unconscious, yet he'd heard her. Had heard the panic in her voice. The need. And that was what had pulled him back from the edge, had allowed him the strength to dispel the water in his lungs.

He would answer her question, but first, she needed to know a few things. "Earlier today, I received a text. It was a picture of you, with blood on your face, tied up, with a gun to your head."

She nodded slowly. "I didn't know who they were sending it to."

"They wanted a trade. Me for you."

"And you said yes?"

"Of course."

"But you didn't contact the police? Why?"

This was where it got complicated. He must have hesitated for too long because she slapped her hand down flat on the table. "Do not lie to me. Please."

He nodded. "First of all, they didn't give me an exact location. They told me to return to Missouri and that I would get further instruction. So I didn't know where to send the police. Even if I had, I wouldn't have taken the chance that they'd screw it up. Not when your life was at stake."

"Where were you?"

"They thought I was in Italy. I had been but I'd left as soon as I was informed of Milo's death. I was in the States hours before they expected me. The element of surprise was in my corner."

"How did you find me?"

This was going to be hard on her. But she'd asked him not to lie. "I contacted your brother-in-law, Bray Hollister. I wanted to know what he knew about your absence. I figured you'd told Summer and that she'd probably told him. I didn't want to go directly to Summer if I didn't have to."

"She's pregnant."

"I know," he said. He smiled. "I'm happy for her."

She gripped her head in her hands as if holding her brains in. "This is surreal. You know all about my life and I know nothing about you."

There was nothing much he could say about that. "Bray said that you were at Heelie Lake and that you'd rented a cottage based on a recommendation from M.A. Fikus.

I went to see her and… Well, you know that part. I still didn't know exactly where you were but I headed for Heelie. I got a lead that Bernie Wilberts owned a lot of cottages in the area and I wanted to identify his properties. I went to his house. His wife…" He stopped, not wanting to tell her. Too much death.

"What?" she demanded.

"Trish, his wife was dead. Shot three times at close range in the back. Just like M.A."

She sucked in a deep breath. "By the men who had me?"

"I don't know. But I'm guessing they had some involvement. What time did they grab you?"

"Just after lunch. A little before one."

"If I had to guess, Mrs. Wilberts was killed several hours before that. Big Tony and Anthony were likely responsible."

"Big Tony?" she repeated. "I heard him call the young one Anthony, so I knew that. I thought they were probably father and son."

"Anthony Sr. and Anthony Jr. Paradini."

"In my head, I called the father Old Guy."

He smiled. "Big Tony probably wouldn't have been happy about that. He dates women who are barely old enough to vote. Spends a lot of money on them. That's usually enough to convince them to stick around for a few months."

"You seem to know a lot about him."

"About seven years ago, I infiltrated the organization he works for."

"*Infiltrated?* Like a spy?" She practically spit the last word.

"Intelligence," he corrected. "For a small agency connected with the United States Department of the Treasury. We protect the financial system."

"You're an accountant?" she asked, doubt in her tone.

She was probably remembering that he didn't even balance his own checkbook. "While we protect the financial system, very few of us actually have accounting or finance backgrounds. I have a master's in biochemical engineering."

"You're a federal agent."

Her tone was bemused. Or maybe that was just his ears ringing.

"I thought you were a construction worker. Every day you packed a lunch and went to work, to build the mall in Hamerton. Or was that a lie, too?"

Her words stung. But it was important to keep going. "I was always good with my hands. When I wanted to stay in Ravesville, that seemed like the best job for me." He paused, closed his eyes. Centered himself. "The night of the storm, I was passing through, with no intent to stay. But something happened between us that night, as we sat on the floor eating pie. And I couldn't go. Because of you, Trish."

He pushed his chair back from the table, the legs scraping on the wood floor. He stood up fast, which was a mistake. It made his head roll. He sank back down. "But you have to know," he said, "that if I thought I was bringing any danger to you, I would never have done it. I thought it was safe. That I was safe."

"I don't understand."

"The people who have the power to *upset* the entire monetary structure that sustains this country are the same people who facilitate terrorist plots, bankroll drugs and deal in weapons of mass destruction," he said. "Seven years ago I successfully infiltrated an organization in the Middle East that we believed was attempting to engineer a biochemical weapon that had the potential to kill millions if released in an urban area under exactly the right conditions."

"They were terrorists," she said.

"Yes. And over a period of three years, I managed to become one of them. My cover was that of a well-educated, financially advantaged, disenfranchised American. Ryan Weber. That was my name. Ivy League college education. High school track star. Born in Connecticut. Parents deceased. Access to substantial trust fund. A whole persona was built, one that would have stood the scrutiny of the best background investigations."

"Ryan Weber." She repeated the name as if she was trying to reconcile everything that he was telling her.

"Ryan Weber worked side by side with them on developing exactly the right formula as well as the right components."

"Components?"

"Something that could be transported easily and not detected. It could be perfect, but if they couldn't get it into the country, it did them no good."

"It wasn't Ryan Weber doing this. It was you helping them." She said it without inflection, her voice sounding dull.

"Every day," he admitted. "And every night, I was transmitting information back to my team, who were supporting me. I was attempting to foil and delay the group's progress in multiple ways, all without them having a clue that I was playing both sides. But I did it. Ultimately, the group decided to make a trial run at an event in England, targeting the London Tube system. We couldn't let it go forward, of course."

"What happened?"

"I continued to play my role. Up until the final moment. Ideally, the principals of the operation needed to be apprehended with the goods on them, so to speak, so that arrests could be made without compromising my involvement."

"And that happened?"

"Yes."

"You say it as if it was no big deal," she said.

It had been a freakin' huge deal and fraught with multiple opportunities for failure. But that was not important now. "Suffice it to say that the necessary arrests were made before the chemical was released. The operation was shut down. People were going to prison with no hope of parole. And I needed to disappear."

"That's when you came to Ravesville?"

"Yes. I returned to the States. I was going to continue my work with the agency but in a domestic position, located on the West Coast. I stopped in Ravesville on my way there. But...well, you know the next part. You weren't going to leave your twin sister and your business. And I...I couldn't leave you. So I made a decision. I contacted my boss, told him I was out."

"All without telling me?"

He'd wanted to. Had wanted her to know that he'd been playing the part of someone else for so long, that he felt like a stranger in his own skin. Had wanted her to know that it was only with her that he felt like Rafe Roper again. "I couldn't. And then nine months after we were married, things started to fall apart. I got word that one of the people on my team had jumped in front of a subway train and been killed. Ruled a suicide but I wasn't convinced. Especially when three months later, a second one was killed when an elevator malfunctioned in his building and fell multiple stories. I knew it couldn't be a coincidence. My old boss said I was imagining things. But I knew our identities had been compromised. I knew that they would come for me. And I wasn't going to take the chance that you'd get caught in the cross fire."

"So you faked your own death."

"I did. And while I desperately wanted to tell you the truth, I knew that I couldn't. You're a genuine person, Trish. You would have struggled to hide the truth from people you loved. Not being able to tell Summer the truth would have eaten at you. And I couldn't do that to you."

"You thought dying would be easier on me?" she asked, as if trying to make sense of the logic.

"Nothing was going to be easy. But if you and everyone else believed I was dead, then you were safer. That was what was important."

"And what was Milo's role? Was he part of your team?"

"Not on this particular project but I'd known him for years. Respected his abilities. He had lots of family money and had retired early. He was happy to watch over you and Summer so that I could do what I needed to do."

"He worked so hard," she said, shaking her head. "I could never have guessed."

"That's why he was perfect. By the way, he loved working with you and Summer. Said that you two were the daughters that he never had."

He could see her swallow hard and realized that of everything he'd told her, that might have been the most difficult for her to hear.

"I had to find out who was behind the attacks on the

team," he continued. "Find out who had compromised all of us. I told my boss I wanted back in. He was reluctant. Said I was coming back for the wrong reasons. Ultimately, I told him I'd go to his boss if necessary, all the way up to the president if necessary."

"The president of the United States?"

"Yes. My fabricated background wasn't all that different from my real background. I did my graduate work at Harvard. The president's son was my roommate when his dad was vice president. I'd been to the West Wing of the White House often enough over the years that I knew how to get a late-night pizza delivered there without it getting hung up in security."

"Amazing," she said, shaking her head.

He understood. Not amazing that he'd been in the West Wing ordering pizza. Amazing that she'd never known any of these things.

"It took me some time but I finally figured out that I wasn't the only one who was a pretty good liar. The entire time that I was working in the Middle East, I had no idea that the organization was financed by a man living in Italy, posing as a winemaker. Luciano Maladucci."

"Someone in Italy, a winemaker, is supporting terrorists?"

She clearly didn't believe him. "There are people all over the world supporting terrorism. People in the United States. People in countries that we consider allies in the fight against terrorism. Everywhere. For all different reasons. Sometimes it's as simple as a screwed-up ideology. This time it was much more basic. Financial. Luciano Maladucci has a significant financial interest in a pharmaceutical company that is developing an antidote to just the kind of chemical weapon we stopped. He stood to make billions."

She said nothing.

His stomach was roiling and he was pretty sure he was about thirty seconds away from losing its contents. He probably did have a concussion. "Listen," he said. "We'll stay here through the night and in the morning make the necessary decisions."

"You still haven't answered my question," she said. "Why did Milo say, 'Tell Rafe they know'?"

"I suspect he meant that the Maladucci family knows that I'm alive."

"Because they still want to kill you?"

"Even more now," he said.

"I don't understand," she said.

He needed to get horizontal. "We can talk tomorrow. I'll take the love seat."

"You're two feet too tall for that," she said.

"It'll be fine," he said.

"For God's sake," she said, her voice shaking. "Just please take the damn bed."

Fine. He couldn't fight about it. He got up more slowly this time and congratulated himself on not falling over.

"But—"

"Can it wait, Trish?" he asked, interrupting her.

She stared at him so intently that he wondered just what she was seeing. Finally, she nodded. "Yes, it can."

TRISH SAT AT the worn kitchen table, staring at the nicks and grooves that the candlelight danced over. She was worried about Rafe. He was putting on a good show but she wasn't fooled. He'd gone into the bathroom and vomited. He'd tried to hide it from her by turning on the water in the sink and the shower, too, but she'd heard the unmistakable sounds of someone retching. Then he'd gone into the bedroom and she'd heard the sounds of the bed creaking as he lowered himself down.

He needed a doctor. Head injuries were tricky. Everybody knew that. She waited another five minutes but couldn't stand it.

She picked up the candle and went to the bedroom door. His eyes were closed. But even ill, he'd heard her. "Yes," he said.

"Why can't we go to the police or to the hospital?" she asked, her words clipped with frustration.

He sighed. "Because right now, I don't know who I can trust. I trust myself and you. Until I figure out who else can be invited into the circle, we stay low."

"We can trust Summer. I think we can trust the Hollisters. They would help us."

"We might be putting them in danger," he said.

She thought of her twin and her unborn baby, of Adie and Keagan. "There has to be someone else," she said.

He didn't answer. After a long minute, she turned around and walked back to the table. She could hear the wind now. It was really blowing. And just then, a crack of lightning broke the sky, visible through the cotton curtains on the windows.

She knew she should be grateful to have shelter. A night on the water in a bad storm would be terrible. And she was suddenly very tired. She'd been tense every single minute of the hours that she'd been tied up and it had taken a toll on her. And she was hungry, too. It had been a long time since her early lunch.

Knowing what was in the refrigerator and that it wasn't much, she opened the freezer. There were a few packages of frozen meat and a loaf of bread. She pulled out a package of bacon and the bread and tossed both of them on the counter.

She felt bad about consuming the Norton's food but she would send them money once she got home.

That thought settled around her like a heavy, wet blanket. She'd left Ravesville less than twenty-four hours ago but it seemed like a lifetime. So much had happened. So many truths revealed.

How could she go back and pretend that Rafe was dead?

It dawned on her that he'd been right about one thing. It would have been very difficult for her to pretend that he was dead when he wasn't. To lie every single day to Summer. That was just not something that she would have been able to do.

But now she would have to do that? Right? She and Rafe hadn't actually talked about that piece of it. Was he going to slip away again to go fight bad guys?

She wanted to know what he was thinking but knew that it would have to wait. The man was injured. She was worried about that. What the hell would she do if he suddenly lapsed into a coma or worse? But he did not intend to seek medical attention. The only thing she could do was wait.

Wait for him to wake up. Wait for him to tell her his plans. Wait for him to leave again.

Wait to be alone again.

She walked back to the doorway of the bedroom. He was stretched out, his breaths deep and even. Just listening to it stirred memories of all the nights she had lain in bed next to him. Listening to him sleep. Her own body humming from making love to him.

She had thought she was the luckiest woman in the world. And then her world had stopped turning on its axis and the ride she was on had come to a jarring stop.

She'd become a widow.

Now, as she walked back out to the small living room and sat on the love seat, she leaned her head back and stared into the darkness. It would not be the first time she'd slept sitting up. For months after Rafe's death, she'd slept in a chair, unable to return to the bed that she'd shared with him.

And as if it had been lurking in the back of her mind, just waiting for the opportunity to pop up, the memory of a joke she'd seen somewhere online came to her. She couldn't remember the joke but the graphic was in her head. An old lady, a cat in her lap, sleeping in her chair, the black hairs on her sagging chin blowing back and forth with the force of her snores.

She thought about the text that she'd sent earlier that day when she'd been eating lunch. She'd done it because she'd finally turned a corner and realized that she didn't have to be alone, pining away for Rafe Roper.

Of course, she hadn't known at the time that Rafe was alive. That she was still married.

Even if it was in name only. And she wasn't the type that could turn her back on that. She had a date next Saturday night. Wasn't that a kick in the pants? First date in four years and she'd made it on the day her dead husband rose from the grave.

She closed her eyes. No time to worry about that right now. She needed to focus on surviving. In the dark cottage, safe from the raging storm, it was peaceful. But in her heart, she knew this was simply a temporary interlude. Danger lurked.

Chapter Thirteen

"Rafe."

It was a whisper of a breath across his cheek. He smiled. This was going to be one of his good dreams.

Over the years, he'd quickly learned to tell the difference. In the good dreams, Trish had been smiling, maybe standing at the counter of the café, coffeepot in hand, pushing a piece of pie in his direction. Or in her blue jeans, planting flowers in their garden, dirt on her cheeks. Or even better, lying naked in their bed, her face flushed with desire.

The bad ones had been Trish at his funeral, her body bent with grief, or Trish lying faceup on some sidewalk, her body lifeless, a bullet hole in her forehead, blood seeping out of her.

When the good dreams came, he would fight to stay asleep, fight to hold the joy. When the bad dreams came, he'd jerk himself awake, no matter how tired, and that would be it for sleep that night. He wouldn't take the chance of sinking back into hell.

"Rafe."

He felt her warm hand on his forehead. Her skin was always so soft, smelled so damn good. Tasted better.

In his really good dreams, he would taste her. Everywhere. And when she came apart, convulsing in his arms, he would lick the sweetness of her body.

"Rafe."

More insistent. Needy. Wonderful.

He reached out, wrapped his hand around her wrist, brought it to his mouth. Touched her with his tongue.

"Hey?" she cried and jerked away.

He opened his eyes and quickly shut them when he was temporarily blinded by the flashlight.

"What the hell was that about?" she asked.

Embarrassment flooded his system. Rafe Roper didn't get caught short. "If you'll get the damn light out of my eyes, it would help," he said, attempting to buy a couple of seconds.

He heard the soft click of it being turned off. Took in two more deep breaths and then opened his eyes. He didn't need any light to know that Trish sat on the edge of his bed. How was it possible that she still smelled of sunshine after the day she'd had?

"I'm sorry," he said. Hell, he should just get it stamped on his forehead.

"Why did you do that?" she asked.

Could he tell her about the dreams? Would it make her feel any better to know that she hadn't been the only one hurting? Was he looking for some sympathy? Like, *Hey, look, I suffered, too.*

That was pretty damn pathetic. "I don't know," he lied.

She snorted, as if to say that she didn't buy it but quite frankly wasn't expecting more out of him. "I was worried about your head injury," she said. "I remembered reading somewhere that the injured person should be awakened every couple of hours."

"I'm going to be fine." He thought that was true. A

few days of rest and he would be good to go. Unfortunately, they didn't have a few days. Much less than that before it would start to fall apart.

His internal clock told him that he'd been sleeping for a couple of hours. The fire at the cottage would have been extinguished but it was likely that they'd still be sifting through the rubble, attempting to identify bodies. He had no idea whether Big Tony or Anthony carried identification on them. He assumed they did.

So it was just a matter of time before word got out that the men were dead. He had to assume that whoever had launched that rocket would be expecting other bodies inside. Trish, for sure. Even in the unlikely event that the attacker hadn't known she was inside, her Jeep was there.

He didn't want to bring it up but he thought that it was entirely possible that Summer had already been notified that her sister was suspected dead. They, of course, wouldn't be able to confirm it without a body.

He wished he'd thrown in his second cell. He wouldn't worry about using it. He was confident that it had never been compromised. He'd considered returning to his rental car to get it but ultimately decided not to in the event that the BMW had been traced to him.

It was a risk to go look for a telephone, but when he'd been driving around this afternoon, he'd passed several marinas and he thought he recalled seeing telephone booths at a couple of them. Throwbacks to a different time. They needed gas for the boat anyway, so perhaps it was a good way to kill two birds with one stone.

It was a bad analogy because right now, he felt as if he and Trish were the birds. Dumb birds, because somebody was just waiting for them to show themselves and then they were going to get blasted.

"Did you sleep?" he asked.

"Some."

He was pretty sure she was lying. "You take the bed," he said, attempting to sit up.

She put her hand flat on his chest and pushed him back. "Oh, please," she said. "I found some bacon and bread."

It was his favorite sandwich. Toasted bread piled high with bacon and a little ketchup. Was she remembering? Or was it just coincidence and he was trying to convince his sorry self that she still cared?

"There wasn't much choice," she said.

That answered that. He closed his eyes. "I'll get something when I wake up the next time. Then we'll take off, look for a phone. Get the lay of the land."

"Are we in trouble here, Rafe? Big trouble?"

He opened his eyes. "It's trouble," he said simply. "But nothing that we can't handle." He sincerely hoped that was true.

"I hope you're not lying to me again," she said. Then got up and left the room.

And he was alone. Again. Still.

TRISH, WHO WOULD have sworn on a stack of Bibles that she couldn't sleep a wink, woke up when a gentle hand shook her shoulder.

"It's morning."

When she and Rafe had been married… Wait—they were still married… Well, when they had been living together, he used to wake her up with *It's morning, darling*. She wondered if he still remembered that.

She opened her eyes and stretched. Her neck hurt from the awkward angle caused by the arm of the love seat.

She pushed herself to a sitting position. Rafe stood in front of her.

It was daylight and he'd opened one of the curtains partway, letting in natural light. It was the best conditions she'd seen him in and he, quite frankly, looked like hell.

His eyes were shadowed with pain, his face was spotted with dried blood that she'd missed with the damp paper towel and he needed a shave. But he seemed steady enough on his feet.

She sniffed and realized it was bacon that she smelled. Somehow he'd managed to cook without her hearing anything. Her stomach growled and she put a hand on it.

He smiled. "Let's eat," he said.

"What time is it?"

"Just after six," he said. "The marina should be open."

"Marina?"

"Yeah. We need gas for the boat and I'm hoping we can find a phone there."

"What can I tell Summer?"

He looked surprised, as if he hadn't expected the question. "Last night, you said that it might be possible that Summer's phone is bugged. I want to make sure I don't say anything stupid to get us into more trouble."

"I appreciate that," he said. He walked over to the counter and pushed four pieces of bread into the toaster. "I think our best bet is to call Chase Hollister."

"Bray is her husband, not Chase."

"I know. But Chase is the police chief. I don't think anybody would have thought to put surveillance on his phone. He can get word to Summer and Bray. Do you know his number?"

She really, really wanted to talk to Summer, wanted to tell her how crazy mixed-up this whole thing was and that she wasn't sure of anything at this point. Summer would understand. But she would do nothing that might put Summer in danger. "I don't know his cell but I know the police station number. I learned it years ago in case there was an emergency at the café. What can I tell him?"

"Reassure him that you're alive and well. Give him permission to tell Summer but make sure he understands that them telling anyone that they've heard from you could further endanger us. And I'd appreciate it if you didn't tell him where you are. I don't want to have to deal with the Hollisters coming here en masse to try to save the day. Then I'll have more people to worry about getting hurt or killed."

He put two sandwiches together, dribbled ketchup on his and nothing on hers, and brought them over, along with a paper towel for each. "The people who own this place must not be coffee drinkers. I couldn't find a pot or any of the fixings."

"Barbarians," she said.

He smiled. He loved coffee as much as she did. "Maybe we can catch a cup at the marina."

"I thought you were worried about me being so recognizable. My hair," she added.

He pointed toward the shelf near the door. "Ball cap. You're going to need to put it up as best you can. And those and some duct tape will add some bulk." He moved his index finger to point at the stack of pillows he'd placed on one of the kitchen chairs.

She pointed to her tank, which maybe wasn't skintight but she sure as hell wasn't getting a pillow under it. "I don't think so."

"There are men's and women's clothing in the bedroom closet. We're going to borrow."

What hadn't he thought of? "You've been busy. How long have you been up?"

"Long enough that I'm fairly confident that I'm not going to fall down." He picked up two of the pillows. "I'll change in the bathroom."

She finished her sandwich and went to examine the closet. She pulled out a large navy blue shirt that buttoned up the front and some gray pants. She felt dumpy just looking at them.

She left her own clothes on but pulled the pants on over them. She zipped and buttoned and gathered the waist. She used her own belt to secure the pants. She was struggling to get the pillows taped into place when the bathroom door opened. Rafe wore a green shirt and pants and the fishing hat that he'd worn in from the boat the previous night. It did a good job of obscuring his cut. He looked twenty pounds heavier.

"Need some help?" he asked.

She didn't want to delay them. "Okay."

He came into the bedroom and stood close. She could smell the soap that he'd used to wash his face and hands. "Just hold them," he said, motioning to the two pillows that she awkwardly clutched above each hip.

She did and he wrapped the duct tape around her body, slipping it under her right arm, around her back, under her left arm, across her breast.

The two pillows didn't quite meet and the tips of his fingers swept across the valley of her breasts. Her thin cotton shirt was barely a barrier. He jerked his head up. "Sorry," he mumbled. He cut the tape and started wrapping again, this time lower, securing the pillows around her stomach.

Higher. She almost begged. Her traitorous breasts remembered his touch and she could feel her nipples tighten in response.

As soon as the tape was secured, she jerked away, turning so that he couldn't see her face. The curse of being a redhead was that she blushed easily—when she was scared or mad or aroused.

With shaking hands, she buttoned up the ugly 1X shirt. Still with her back toward him, she reached both arms up, separated her long hair into three different sections and efficiently braided it. When she was done, she secured the braid with a rubber band that she'd found in the kitchen drawer.

Finally, she turned to him. His mouth was slightly open, his gaze fixed. He was standing perfectly still except that the thumb on his right hand was rubbing against his index and middle fingers.

And she felt heat in her core, knowing that she wasn't the only one in the room experiencing ill-timed lust.

"Trish," he said, sounding needy.

It would be so easy to slip back, to forget the pain that she'd battled through these past four years. "I have a date on Saturday," she blurted out. "I've moved on."

Someone not familiar with Rafe would have thought the news had no impact upon him. But she saw the subtle shift in his dark eyes.

"Who's the lucky guy?" he asked casually, as if he was asking about the weather.

"No one that you would know."

"From Ravesville?" he asked.

"No."

"How did you meet him?"

He'd given up his right to ask questions four years ago. "None of your business," she said.

He shrugged, turned and walked out of the bedroom. He picked up the baseball hat on the shelf and, without looking at her, tossed it in her direction.

She put on the hat, hoping that it would keep her brain stuffed into place because clearly it had to be rattling around right now, muddying up the clear connection between thought and emotion.

She didn't like people who were deliberately hurtful. Tried to avoid them. But lashing out had been infinitely better than asking him to touch her, to kiss her, to make love to her.

Still, she had a very sour taste in her mouth.

It would take more than coffee to wash it away.

"Do you have your gun?" Rafe asked.

She walked over and pulled it out from beneath the love seat cushion. "I'm not sure how to carry it. Especially now. These pants are too loose. If I stick it in the waistband, it might fall through and I'll end up shooting off my foot."

He pointed to the pockets. "Use those. If you need to shoot, don't worry about pulling your gun out. Just stick your hand in your pocket, flip off the safety and aim in the general direction of the bad guy."

"How will I know who the bad guy is?"

"He'll be the person trying to kill us."

There wasn't a hint of humor in his tone. "I should be able to figure that out, then," she said. She put the gun in her pocket. It weighed down her pants on one side, and if someone looked really closely at her, they might put two and two together and come up with locked and loaded. "I'm ready."

He pointed at the two pairs of sunglasses that were on

the shelf next to the door. "Take whichever pair fits the best. I'll take the other."

He waited while she tried both and selected one. When he put his glasses on, he really didn't look much like Rafe anymore.

His hand was on the door, but for some reason, he wasn't turning the knob. Finally, he turned toward her. "I don't want to take you," he said. "But I can't leave you here by yourself, either. There's no damn safe place."

She didn't want to stay at the cottage. As mad as she was at Rafe, she felt safer with him. "Let's go," she said. "It'll be fine. As long as the marina has coffee, that is."

HE HADN'T BEEN kidding when he'd said that he didn't want to take her. But leaving her was not an option. He couldn't protect her if he was halfway across the lake. They would stick together.

For now, he realized. *I've moved on.*

Those words had been like a knife to the gut. Which was ridiculous. Wasn't that what he'd wanted? Wasn't that what he'd told Milo time and time again? Insisted. *Find someone for her*, he'd said. *I don't want her to be alone.*

Hadn't he given up every damn thing so that she could be safe?

He supposed that might be the fundamental problem. They both saw themselves as the aggrieved party. There wasn't much to be gained by playing the I-hurt-more-than-you game.

The lake was quieter than his tumultuous thoughts, yet still not empty. With the naked eye, he could see five other boats. Probably fishermen wanting to get an early start. Hopefully not anyone looking for them.

When Trish headed for the back of the boat, he pointed

to the passenger seat up front. He wanted her close in case something happened.

Once she was seated, he started the engine and pulled away from the dock. He was satisfied that she was disguised as well as he could have hoped. The pillows and the big clothing made her look overweight and sort of sloppy. She'd stuffed her braided hair up inside the ball cap. As long as it stayed there, they might just pull this off.

If it had been only Trish's need to communicate with Summer, he might have held the line and told her that it was simply going to have to wait. But he needed to get out, to start gathering intelligence, to figure out what the heck had happened last night.

He drove the boat to the middle of the lake, far enough away from shore that from there it would be hard to distinguish their features without good binoculars. He kept his speed steady, not too slow, not too fast. Ten minutes later, he saw the marina. Now there was no choice but to return to shore.

There were three people visible on the dock. One, a young man, maybe twenty-five, wearing a white T-shirt and gray shorts, holding a clipboard. He was waving his arms toward a row of boats, as if to tell the young couple he was facing that they could have their choice of craft.

The woman pointed at what appeared to be a sweet twenty-six-foot Rendezvous and the couple climbed in. While Clipboard Guy was busy giving them last-minute instructions, Rafe docked the boat and tied up. With his index finger, he discreetly pointed at her, then at the pay phone that was ten feet away from the marina office. Trish did not acknowledge the instruction. He wasn't sure she was breathing.

"Relax," he said under his breath. "We're just a couple out for an early morning fishing trip. No reason for anybody to think anything different." He waited until she gave him a jerky nod before stepping out of the boat. He held out a hand for Trish.

She took it and he realized her fingers were ice-cold. He wanted to assure her that everything was going to be fine, but since she'd asked him not to lie to her anymore, he wasn't going to offer up any assurances that might not be true.

"I don't have any money," she said when she was standing close to him.

He'd thought of that. He had cash but he thought there might be another way that would ensure the call got answered. "Make it a collect call. Tell the operator that you're Raney Hollister."

"That's Chase's wife. How do you know that?" she asked, her eyes wide.

"That's probably not the most important thing right now. Chase will accept the call." He added, "I'll get the gas and then go inside for the coffee."

He was surprised when he didn't have to prepay for the gas. Showed how much people in this area still trusted.

And speaking of trust, it was a risk letting her talk to Chase without him listening in. She might unconsciously give away their location. Might do it on purpose, he realized. He wasn't confident that she trusted him.

Or would ever trust him again.

But the only hope of getting them back on the right path was to show that he trusted her. With an eye still on her, he dragged the gas hose away from the pump and stuck it into the boat's tank. She had the phone up to her ear with her back to him.

She was still talking when the automatic shutoff clicked off. The young couple were in their boat now, putting on their life jackets. Clipboard Guy was about to untie them.

He put the gas cap back on and walked toward the marina shop. When he opened the door of the shop, he could smell freshly brewed coffee and knew that the trip wasn't going to be a total bust. There was no one else inside, not even a clerk. Clipboard Guy must handle the whole show during the early mornings.

Rafe wondered around the small space. There were only three aisles. He found some bug spray and sunscreen, which he figured could come in handy. He remembered how easily Trish burned. He picked up a gallon of milk and was studying the candy bars in the small freezer at the front of the store when the young man entered.

"Morning," Rafe said. "Going to be another hot one." The weather was always a safe topic.

"Ninety-two," said the kid. He walked behind the cash register and leaned his butt against the back counter.

Rafe walked away from the freezer and set what he had in his arms on the counter before moving on to the coffeemaker in the middle of the room. "Smells good," Rafe said, nodding his head at the pot. "Outside, it smells like somebody had a big bonfire."

"Did you see it?" the kid asked, his eyes wide.

Rafe shook his head. "Just rolled into town this morning."

"Well, then you missed the most excitement this place has had in years. A cottage blew up, just exploded. And then, just like in the movies, two cars caught on fire and they blew up, too. One of them was a sweet black BMW. That had to be fifty thousand just up in smoke."

When they'd left the cottage the first time, there had

been only Trish's Jeep in the driveway. Somebody driving a BMW had arrived in that twenty minutes that they'd been gone. "Anybody get hurt?" Rafe asked, picking up a package of powdered doughnuts.

"I'll say. Three people are dead. I heard that they can't even tell if they are men or women."

He knew two of them were men. Big Tony and Anthony. He wasn't sure about the mystery guest. "That can't be good for tourism."

"I know. My mom works for the county dispatch center. She talks to the cops all the time," he said proudly. "They think they know one of the people. His license plate survived the blast. They went..." The kid hesitated, as if he knew that he shouldn't be repeating something that his mom had discussed at home.

Rafe turned, just far enough that he could see Trish getting back into the boat. He listened for the engine, thinking it was possible that she might try to leave him there. But it was quiet.

He added a bag of popcorn to the stuff already on the counter. He pulled out a hundred-dollar bill. "This plus $68.20 at the pump. They went?" he prompted.

"The police. When they went to his house to tell his wife, she was already dead. Shot in the back."

Was it possible that more than one woman had been shot in the back in this small community? He didn't think so. The third person in the cottage had to be Bernie Wilberts.

"The cops found the woman's phone and there was a text on it from her husband saying that he was going to be home soon, that he was stopping at their rental cottage first. They said it came in around eight o'clock but that she never would have gotten it. She was already stiff."

He said it as though it was no big deal. It made him think of how Trish hated it when her nephew, Keagan, played violent video games. She said it was ruining young people, making them desensitized to violence.

"I imagine the police will figure it out."

"My mom said they're getting some help from the state. Forensics. Maybe somebody like Abby from *NCIS*."

He'd seen the show. Over the years, he'd worked with a dozen Abbys but none that ever wore roller skates. "That would be cool."

The kid handed him his change and then put the two large coffees in a cardboard carrier. The rest of the items went into a white plastic sack.

Rafe opened the door of the shop. But before he could step outside, he saw the boat, idling at low speed. A hundred yards out from the far edge of the dock. Two men, both midforties, both with dark hair. One had twenty pounds on the other, but besides that, they were eerie replicas of each other. He did not recognize either one of them. And while they were dressed as fishermen, there was something not quite right about their appearance. Their clothes looked brand-new.

They were studying Trish, who had her back to them.

Chapter Fourteen

Rafe forced himself to stay put. He got ready to lose the coffee that he was carrying in his right hand. The milk and other purchases were in a sack, looped over his left wrist. He mentally adjusted for the slight difference in his center of gravity.

He was an excellent shot. But two against one were never good odds in a gunfight. Four years ago, Trish had been a decent shot. He'd made sure of that. But by the time she figured out what was going on and got to her gun, it would be over.

The two men looked at one another and one shook his head. They revved up their engine and moved toward the open water.

Rafe let out his breath. The kid at the marina wouldn't have been able to stop talking for weeks if there had been a gunfight on his dock.

"You okay, man?" asked the kid, from behind him.

"Yes," Rafe said without turning around. He watched the men. They were picking up speed, moving quickly away.

He moved out of the doorway and walked the length of the dock. He stepped into the boat and handed Trish the coffee carrier. She removed both cups and handed him back one.

"I spoke to Chase," she said.

He wanted to demand to know what she'd said but he didn't ask. Just untied the boat, started the engine and pulled away from the dock. When they were fifty yards out, he opened the sack, pulled out the bag of powdered doughnuts and gently tossed them in Trish's lap.

"I found out something," she said.

"Me, too. You first."

ME, TOO. YOU FIRST. It was their game. It would usually start within minutes of both of them getting home from work in the evening. They would be in the kitchen, working on dinner. One of them would start by saying *I saw something interesting today* or *I heard something funny today* or *I did something for the first time today.* The other one would automatically have to say *Me, too. You first.*

And it would begin. Laughing and talking about their day. Most nights they would end up in bed before dinner could be cooked.

Sharing everything.

Well, not everything. That was obvious now. She pushed those ugly thoughts away. "You were right. The local police tracked my license plate back to Ravesville and contacted Chase."

"I imagine he was surprised to hear from you."

He had been grateful but not that surprised. "The officer he spoke with confirmed that my body had not been identified. That, along with whatever it was you said to Bray, must have been enough for them to keep positive."

"Had he told Summer?"

"No. He and Bray made the decision not to. But they're going to tell her now that they know I'm okay."

"Did he want to know where you are?"

"Yes. But I told him that I'd promised you that I wouldn't say."

He turned to stare at her. "Thank you," he said.

"He wasn't very happy about that, so I did tell him that I'd check in tomorrow, too."

"Okay, we'll make that happen."

She opened the bag of doughnuts. "The cop told Chase that there were *three* people in the cottage."

"I know. The kid at the marina told me the same thing. They tentatively identified one as Bernie Wilberts, based on his license plate. Same as they did for you."

The doughnut tasted chalky in her mouth and she washed it down with a big swig of too-hot coffee. It was crazy, really. She'd met the man only once, had one additional telephone conversation, but she felt as if she'd lost someone that she knew well.

Maybe it was because of what Rafe had told her about Mrs. Wilberts. A whole family had been wiped out in one day. "So it was bad timing on his part?" she asked.

Rafe didn't answer. That made her nervous. "What are you thinking?" she demanded.

"The kid at the marina told me that Bernie Wilberts drove a black BMW. I was also driving that same kind of car. I think it's very possible that when Bernie got there, somebody mistook him for me, and the cottage was attacked."

Rafe and Bernie Wilberts didn't look anything alike. Did they? Both had dark hair. Same height. Approximately the same weight. Rafe was all hard muscle, and Bernie... Well, not so much. But from a distance...

The morning wind was picking up and their boat was stirring the water. She watched the trail of wake. It was how her brain felt. Insubstantial. Frothy. But one thing was clear. "Then what you're saying is that you were the target. Not Big Tony or Anthony or me." It was a warm sunny day and a chill ran down her spine.

She had preferred it when she thought she might be the target. Rafe had just come back from the dead. Sort of. And she was very, very angry with him about his deception.

But she couldn't bear to lose him again.

They were nearing the cottage. "Now what?" she asked.

"Let's get out of sight until I figure out what to do next."

He had his hand splayed across his forehead, as if protecting his eyes from the bright sun. He was wearing the clunky sunglasses that he'd found at the cottage but she suspected the quality was poor. He'd probably started the day out with a headache and this couldn't be helping it. But maybe there were details that needed attention before they returned to the cottage. "You said you were driving a car. Where is it?"

"In town, in the public lot near one of the boat rental places."

"Can it be traced to you?"

He shook his head. "This boat either. I rented it under the name Bill Wood."

"They didn't make you show an ID?"

"I have one."

Of course he did. He probably had four or five different IDs in his pocket. This husband of hers that she really truly didn't know. "Pretty soon nothing you say will surprise—"

She heard the noise a millisecond before she hit the floor of the boat with Rafe's big body covering her. She managed to raise her head.

Rafe already had a gun in his hand, his own head raised, scanning the horizon. His body was taut with barely contained energy.

She heard the sound again and was able to track the origin. A boat on the near shore, its engine backfiring. She realized Rafe had come to the same conclusion when he moved off her and extended a hand to help her up.

"Sorry," he mumbled.

Maybe he was full of surprises. Maybe there were a thousand sides that she had yet to see. But this man would protect her. He would give up his own life to save hers.

That spiked an emotion that she wasn't ready yet to deal with and she turned away from him.

SECONDS AGO, WHEN the damn boat had backfired, his first thought had been that the two men in the boat had somehow circled back without him noticing and had decided that they'd missed something the first time. He needed Trish to be aware that danger might be very close. "There's something you should know."

She had turned away from him and for a second he thought that maybe she was giving him a message that she was done listening, that she'd heard about all she could handle. But slowly she swiveled in her seat.

"I saw two men in a boat this morning. They cruised past the marina. I thought they were giving you a close look."

She motioned to herself. "In these clothes with an extra forty pounds, there's not much to look at."

"You could dress in a gunnysack and you'd be beautiful," he said.

Her fair complexion colored fast. She wasn't used to receiving compliments. That was his fault. That and so much more.

"Did you recognize them?" she asked.

"No. But they weren't fishermen," he said. "I suspect they're hired help. They'd been given a description of a slender, red-haired woman and they couldn't see past a big blue shirt. That tells me they aren't very smart. Or motivated. Or maybe either."

They could be as dumb as rocks, but still, seeing them that close to Trish, with her unaware, had been almost too much.

What if they'd been just a little smarter? What if they'd been told to shoot first and ask questions later?

He swallowed. The morning sun felt too hot on his face, even though his hat provided shade. The water seemed very blue. Maybe it was the cheap glasses. But then he saw a slim piece of red hair that had escaped from Trish's tight braid. It swung in the breeze, caressing her neck, like a single spike of fire.

Everything was exaggerated. Especially the need that raced through his body. He turned away from Trish, not wanting her to be able to look too close. She had always been able to see too much.

He tied up, scanning the area while he did so. He didn't see anything that concerned him. But then again, a rifle with a scope didn't necessarily require close proximity. He needed Trish inside, with at least the benefit of solid walls.

Not that that had helped Bernie Wilberts all that much.

He just needed to make sure that nobody discovered that they were holed up at the Norton cottage.

He slowed the boat and expertly pulled in next to the dock. After he tied up, he turned to Trish.

"Do you mind carrying these?" he asked, very formally, nodding his head toward the sack of groceries and the still-full coffee cups. "I'd like to keep my hands free."

"Of course," she said, just as formally, as if they were two strangers. Certainly not as if they had been close once, as close as people could be.

He led the way, his gun in hand. When they got to the short grass, he held up his free hand, stopping her. Turning, he whispered, "Let me check it. Run like hell if you hear anything odd."

He crossed the space from the tree line to the back door, a flashback from the night before at the edge of his thoughts. He was confident that he'd not been followed either last night or this morning...but still.

But he got to the door without incident. Then he was inside. The cottage had not been touched. Within seconds, literally, he was back at Trish's side. "All clear," he said.

She didn't answer.

"Are you okay?" he asked.

She made a deliberate look to the right, then the left. "Another day in paradise. What's to complain about?" she snapped.

A small smile escaped before he shut it down. Trish had always hid her nerves with sarcasm. It was silly but just seeing that that one thing hadn't changed made him feel good.

He opened the door to the cottage and let her go inside first. She set the milk down on the counter with a thud. The bug spray rolled out of the sack and onto the tile floor. "Maybe I'd be better," she said, "if I understood what the hell was going on."

He sat down at the table and took off his hat and sunglasses. He desperately wanted to lie down and close his eyes. But she'd given him a pass last night. "There are some things that haven't exactly made sense over the years. And now I think I might know why. I told you last night that we were successful in stopping the London Tube incident and that arrests were made. There were two brothers that were both charged with terrorism-related offenses, all punishable by many years in prison."

"What doesn't make sense about that?" she asked.

"I knew they were brothers. But the whole time that I was working alongside of them, I thought that they did not have other family. No one else was ever mentioned, nor did my team ever identify any other family. And believe me, we're pretty damn thorough. For us to miss that was a big miss."

"How did you find out that it was missed?"

"After my two teammates were killed and I went back to the agency, I started investigating. There's an old rule. Follow the money. And that's what I did. That's when I was finally able to connect the two that we'd arrested with the person who had to have been bankrolling the operation."

"The winemaker in Italy," she said.

"Yes. But I was shocked to learn that the winemaker wasn't just the money guy—he was their father. He'd never been married to the mother. She'd ultimately married someone else. The two sons had been raised by their mother and stepfather."

"But somehow got reunited again with their biological father."

"Shortly after finishing college, we think."

"Last night, you said something about the fact that the Maladucci family had more reason now than ever to come after you."

"Mr. Maladucci had two more sons with a second wife. What we've been able to discover is that one of them has picked up where his older half brothers left off."

"A real family business," she said.

"We're pretty confident that the youngest brother, Demí, is not involved. He's a well-known European philanthropist. But Mario, the older brother, is his father's right hand. I was successfully able to convince one of the secretaries in his office to help me—"

"Did you sleep with her?" she asked, her voice hard.

It knocked him back. "What?"

"In your little cloak-and-dagger world, isn't that how things are done? People trade sex for favors."

She was right. Sometimes. He held up a finger. "I did not sleep with her." But the secretary had slept with Mario. She claimed it was a small price to pay for justice.

Trish braced her elbow on the table and rested her forehead in the palm of her hand. "I'm sorry," she said. "I don't know where that came from."

He understood. Her nerves had to be brittle. In the span of two days, she'd seen Milo killed, Duke shot, been kidnapped, had a husband come back from the dead, heard about multiple people with gunshots to their backs, and was now being told that it was likely worse than what she'd imagined. She was probably hanging on by a thread. And when that happened, people lashed out. And her accusation wasn't unreasonable.

But it still hurt that she could so easily conjure up the accusation. What other things was she thinking but hadn't yet voiced?

He probably didn't want to know. "I convinced her to help me after I uncovered that her brother was killed in a café bombing in France. I thought she might be sympathetic to my efforts and I was right. Luciano and his older son have picked up where the two older half brothers left off. They don't have the technical knowledge but they've hired that expertise. It's more of the same. Another biochemical attack."

"Do you know where?" she whispered.

"At the Kentucky Derby. Opening ceremonies."

She gasped. "That's just a few weeks away."

"I know. And we were moving swiftly. Arrests of Luciano and Mario Maladucci would have been made by the end of next week. That's why I don't think the timing of this is coincidental. Somehow, I think they found out."

"How?"

"That's the big question. Maybe the secretary decided that it was too big of a risk and she confessed her involvement. I don't know. There are always loose ends in operations like this. Of course, this is not the only case I've worked on during the last four years. There have been many others. There is no lack of people doing bad things in this world and I have made some enemies. But from the very beginning, this felt personal. The attack on Milo. Taking you hostage. Somebody wants me to know that they can get to the people that I hold dear. My family, so to speak. I believe it's revenge for what I've brought down on their family. Maybe a counterattack. Maladucci may know that the agency is close to dismantling his operation once again and he's striking first."

"Would the secretary have known that? Would she have been privy to that information?"

"Not from me. And maybe it wasn't her. Maybe it was someone else."

SHE COULD HEAR it in his voice. He was angry. Hurt. She understood. Being deceived by someone you trusted was like a knife in the gut. She thought better, however, of pointing out her observation.

They would deal with their personal situation. One way or another. But in order to have that opportunity, they both needed to stay alive. And based on what Rafe was telling her, there was somebody determined to make sure that didn't happen.

"Do you know who?"

"No. But somewhere along the way, I've trusted the wrong person. Made a mistake."

She sipped her coffee. "You said before that Big Tony and Anthony were owned by the Maladuccis."

"They are little fish," he said. "Anthony probably accepted that. He had much smaller ambitions than his father, much to his father's disappointment. They were muscle supporting a strong revenue stream derived from the sale of illegal drugs and gambling. Maybe a little human trafficking thrown in. You'd be surprised at how diversified these organizations are. Makes Wall Street look like a bunch of amateurs."

Muscle. "I think you might be right. When they took that awful cell phone picture of me, they said something about you not being able to stay away. I didn't know who they were talking about, of course. But Big Tony said something along the lines that it wasn't about me, that it was about making things right."

"Big Tony always had a way with words. Or at the very least, a big mouth."

"So here's what I don't understand. If Big Tony and Anthony were following somebody's orders to kidnap me and kill you, then why blow up the cottage with them in it. That doesn't make sense."

"Agreed."

"So what are the possibilities?" she asked.

"I've settled on these three," he said. "It was somebody who had it out for Big Tony and Anthony, and anybody else who happened to be in the cottage was collateral damage. You, me, Bernie Wilberts. They probably didn't care."

She waited. If he really thought that, they wouldn't be puffing themselves up with pillows and pretending to be Ma and Pa Fisherman.

"Or," he said, "it was somebody in Big Tony and Anthony's infrastructure who wasn't confident that they could get the job done and decided to take matters into his or her own hands."

"In that case," she said, "they were collateral damage. And when it becomes known that we weren't killed, the bad guys are going to keep at it."

"Yes. I imagine so." He rocked his chair back and reached to snag the popcorn off the counter. He opened it and extended it in her direction. She shook her head. Maybe his stomach wasn't a wreck. He lived in this world but her world was eggs over easy and a stack of pancakes. Simple.

"What's the third possibility?" she said.

"A slight variation from door number two, but in this version, the bad guy isn't part of the Maladucci organization. He's a part of my organization." He pushed back his chair and started pacing around the small room. "I've been wondering why now. I've been back with the agency for four years. I didn't think anybody knew about you. But I could have been wrong. You've been in Ravesville the whole time. Why now is there a need to lure you here so that I'll follow? It could have happened anytime in the past four years. Why now?" He tossed back the handful of popcorn and chewed.

It indeed was something to chew on. "Who knew you were close to bringing down the Maladucci family again? This time probably for good."

"Only a handful of people. Hell, not even that. Two trusted coworkers, Daltry and Miara. My boss, Kevin. His boss, Michelle. I suppose even her boss, but since that's the president of the United States, I'm taking that off the table. Four people. Two men, two women."

"Tell me more about them," she said. "These four."

"I've worked with Daltry and Miara since rejoining the agency four years ago. I like both of them, trust both of them."

"As much as the two partners who were killed?" she asked.

He shook his head. "I didn't let myself get that close."

She had figured as much.

"Both Daltry and Miara were part of the surveillance team on the Maladucci house. So they were aware that I abruptly left the property. I told them I wasn't feeling well. They might have wondered about that, but I'm not known for skipping out of work, so they probably would have cut me some slack."

"What about your boss?"

"Kevin Leonard has been my supervisor for a long time. Before I came to Ravesville and then after. He's just a little older than me. We have a good partnership. He doesn't like fieldwork, hates to get his hands dirty. But he's really good at reporting and relationship-building, all the things that I find tedious. He likes wearing suits and his shoes are always polished."

She smiled at the last part. "That's very helpful to know." She considered what he'd told her. "Does he also think you're ill?"

"Yes. Once I'd made the decision to leave Italy, I called him and told him that I wasn't feeling well and would likely be out for several days."

"Was he okay with that?"

"I think he was concerned. Putting the Maladucci family on ice is sort of a big deal. It will get some attention from people higher up in the agency, maybe from even outside the agency. He's ambitious. Smart. I'm sure he wants it to go smoothly and end well. He wants all hands on deck. I could tell that he was a little upset or maybe nervous. He stutters a little when that happens."

"And his boss, Michelle?"

"I rarely interact with her."

"What about support personnel. Surely these people have administrative assistants and things like that. Maybe it's more than four?"

"It's possible, but there is certain work that gets done that is so confidential that it is not shared with support personnel. All correspondence is directed on secure lines only to the intended recipient. Messages can't be copy and pasted, can't be forwarded."

"That doesn't prevent somebody from inviting another person into their office and letting them read over their shoulder."

"You're right about that."

"And what about the computer people? Everybody knows that the people who are responsible for the computer system can see anything they really want to see."

"It's possible, but quite frankly, lots of the messaging was done on secure phone lines and never put in writing."

She sighed. "This is complicated. I don't have a concussion and even I have a headache."

"I'll figure it out," he said. "I have to."

Chapter Fifteen

He needed to check his phone. If somebody had been trying to reach him it might give him one more clue as to who was interested in knowing whether he'd survived the explosion. But he could not check it from here.

Heelie Lake was a big lake. He could take the boat several miles south and put his cell phone battery back in there. If they caught the signal, he'd be long gone before they could get someone in the area. Unless the two guys he'd seen at the marina just got lucky and were close by.

He needed to take the chance. But he did not want to leave Trish, who, even now, probably didn't understand the gravity of their situation.

"I'm guessing that the two we saw on the lake are not the only two looking for us," he said. "It's possible that there are people in multiple places, both on the water and land."

She seemed to consider this as she studied her hands. "You need to use me," she said finally. "To flush them out. We need to find them, demand to know who they're working for. We need to hunt them down, rather than the other way around. I'll show myself," she added, as if she was discussing a walk in the park.

"No," he said. "Absolutely not."

"You said it yourself. They're looking for me. But I'm the small fish. According to your own theories, this probably isn't about me. It's you they want. They aren't going to hurt me. They'll want to use me, to lead them to you."

"They'll still kill you," he said. "Once you've done what they needed."

"We'll have to figure out a way to stop that," she said.

He was always the one with nerves of steel. And now she was the one showing the guts. He hated this but it made sense. Still. "I can't let you do it," he said. He would not, could not, take a chance with her life. But neither could he send her back to Ravesville. The Hollisters would protect her, likely with their lives, but their attacker had already shown that he or she was ruthless and didn't care about others getting hurt.

It was a damn mess. "I can't let you," he said.

"That's ridiculous," she said.

"It's not," he said, barely keeping control of his patience.

"You're not listening to reason. Why can't I do this?" she pushed.

Because he loved her. *I'm moving on.* "Just because, damn it."

The words hung in the air.

"We have to figure out if those two men were indeed looking for me and if so, how many more might be scattered around the area."

"They aren't going to just volunteer the information, Trish," he said.

"We have to figure out a way to convince them to talk to us," she said. "I don't think we should lead them back here. So far, this seems like a pretty safe place for us."

"Agreed."

"I might know a place. I've stayed at the other end of the lake several times. On the west side, it's developed. On the east side, there are a series of small coves. There aren't any cottages because it's federal ground in that area. So it can be pretty isolated."

"What are you proposing?" he asked.

"We take Bernie Wilberts's boat there. It's slower but I think it's in our best interests to keep our boat under wraps as much as possible so that when we're disguised, we feel comfortable driving it."

He tilted his chin down to look at her. "Are you sure you haven't done undercover work?"

She ignored the question. "I'll drop you off and then I make myself visible. Maybe I can do a little shopping on-shore. Hopefully the two men you saw this morning are still in the area. Once I've done that, I'll head back your direction. When they follow me, you can deal with them."

SHE MADE IT sound so simple. But there were a thousand things that could go wrong. The Maladucci family had a lot to lose. Desperate people did stupid things. But hiding out and doing nothing was not his style. And it wasn't making her any safer. "If we do this, I don't want you out of your boat," he said.

"Will you trust me to do what I need to do?" she asked.

Well, hell. "I have always trusted you," he said. He had trusted that she would have the spirit to go on. That alone had kept him sane more than a few nights.

He trusted her enough that he was going to tell her about Henri. Not another living soul knew about him.

"We may have one ace up our sleeve," he said. He told her the story of Henri and how he'd met him. And that he'd stepped in and impersonated him before. He was not specific about the times or the reasons.

When he was finished, she looked a little amused. "So it freaked you out to see your double?" she asked.

"A little. But he's been extraordinarily helpful. There is one pretty significant limitation, however. He's German and doesn't speak English well. He understands it better than he speaks it. So he would never pass for me if it required him to interact with someone. But I think there's a way we can go with your idea to use you as bait." He stopped and shook his head. He hated even saying the word. "And use my relationship with Henri, who is right now cooling his heels somewhere outside St. Louis until he gets word from me."

"I'm ready," she said.

"First, we need to get Henri here. I need to make contact with him. Let's go back to that pay phone at the marina."

TWENTY MINUTES LATER, Rafe finished his call to Henri. He'd been a little afraid the man wouldn't answer the call because it hadn't come from Rafe's second phone. But he had and the conversation had been relatively easy.

Carrying out the plan would be significantly harder.

Before he got back into the boat, he went inside and purchased two large coffees. A different young man was working and barely spoke to him.

When he got back to the boat, Trish smiled at the coffee. "Thank you," she said.

"I knew that one cup earlier wasn't going to cut it," he said, starting the boat.

"Well, what did he say?" Trish asked, her tone impatient.

"He can be here in two hours. I asked him to trailer a boat so that he doesn't have to rent one once he gets here. Less chance of someone seeing him. He'll meet us on the west end of the lake. He'll be wearing a red baseball hat and a white T-shirt."

"I hope there aren't a lot of Cardinals fans on the lake," she muttered.

"Let's hope he's got a strong bat and we knock it out of the park," Rafe answered.

She stared at him, her green eyes intense. He realized that she'd forgotten her sunglasses. "That was fun when you played softball," she said.

His first and only summer in Ravesville, he joined the men's softball team that played at the local park. They'd needed a third baseman. After being undercover for many years and continuously living on the edge, he'd enjoyed the easy camaraderie that existed between the players. Had loved looking up in the stands and seeing Trish cheering for him.

Had looked forward to going home with her those nights and making love to her. And she would tease him in bed. *Make it a good throw, Roper.* And when she would come apart in his arms and he would follow her over the edge, he would whisper in her ear, *Home run for Roper.*

"Trish," he said, his voice sounding rusty.

"Yes," she murmured.

"We have two hours until we have to meet Henri. I...I want you."

She'd asked him to be honest. He couldn't get much more brutally frank than that. He braced himself for her refusal. *I've moved on.*

She made him wait. Then she gave him a half smile. "I've got an idea for the seventh-inning stretch."

His damn heart flipped over in his chest. Just flipped over.

He pushed the speed up another five miles per hour and hummed "Take Me Out to the Ball Game" all the way back to the cottage.

ONCE THEY WERE safely inside the cottage, he caught her in his strong arms and pulled her tight to his body. He smelled like the lake and the coffee that he'd just drunk. His skin was warm and she ran her hands up his arms, over his biceps, across his chest.

And then he bent his head and he kissed her. Consumed her, his mouth greedy, his tongue stabbing into her mouth. With a hand on each side of her face, he held her tight.

Not that she had any intention of pulling away. They were in danger. Someone wanted to kill Rafe, maybe her, too. If they didn't both survive this, she would not have wasted this day, this time.

Still kissing him, she tried to unbutton her ugly blue shirt. She wanted it and the pillows and everything else gone. She wanted to touch him, skin to skin.

He lifted his head. His eyes were dark. "Need some help?" he asked, his tone guttural.

She nodded.

He put a hand on each side of the shirt and ripped. Buttons flew everywhere. "I'll leave them enough money for three shirts," he said, his mouth close to her ear. Then he was licking her collarbone.

And she felt as if the pillows and duct tape were strangling her. There was such need in her body.

"Get a knife," she moaned.

"Kinky, huh?" he teased. He put his hands on her butt and pulled her against him. He was rock hard.

"Rafe Roper," she said, "if you don't get these awful pillows off me in the next ten seconds, I...I don't know what I'm going to do," she finished weakly when he stuck his hand down the front of her baggy pants and touched her.

Even though her cotton capris and her thin panties still separated them, her body responded, as it always had, to his touch.

He knew what she liked.

All was fair in love and war. She unbuckled his belt, unbuttoned his jeans, pulled at the zipper. Started to drop to her knees.

He groaned and held her up. "You win, darling," he said, his mouth against her neck. He put his hands under her bottom and boosted her up. She wrapped her legs around his waist.

And on the way to the bedroom, he snagged the scissors off the table.

Chapter Sixteen

She must have slept. Because when she woke up, she was on her side, with Rafe spooned around her. He had one arm draped over her stomach, her hair curled around his hand.

It had been fast. Electric. Nerve endings that maybe weren't dead but certainly asleep had jumped and saluted. She came minutes after he'd entered her and he'd pounded into her, his wonderful body slick with sweat.

They had not used protection. Hadn't discussed it. But even now, the knowledge that a child could have been created was almost overwhelming. When she'd believed Rafe dead, the thing she had mourned the most was that she hadn't been pregnant. She would never hold one of Rafe's children in her arms.

But now. Maybe.

"Are you awake?" he asked softly, his mouth close to her ear.

"Yes."

"Everything okay?"

She turned to face him. She studied him. "Your cut looks better but the bruise on your forehead is worse."

"I'm fine," he said. He stroked her shoulder. "Are you avoiding the question?"

She stared at his sexy brown eyes and ran the pad of her thumb over his right eyebrow. "I'm not sure everything is okay but I have no regrets," she said.

He sighed but didn't push her for a better explanation, and for that she was grateful. Her emotions were all over the place. Making love to Rafe again had been amazing but there was so much unresolved between the two of them. While he might have had his reasons, and they might even have been good reasons, to have left her and let her believe him dead for four years was not something that someone got over easily.

And then, of course, there was the small matter that someone was trying to kill one or both of them. "Can we talk about next steps?" she asked.

He rolled onto his back and put one arm under his head. The other he kept securely around her. "Sure."

Which was nice and agreeable but his actions weren't matching his words. He was gently rubbing his fingers up and down her naked stomach. His tanned skin was a stark contrast to her very pale skin.

"Stop—that tickles," she said, stilling his hand. It did but it also was distracting—making her think of all the places that she wanted those fingers to go, all the ways he had made her come in the past without ever taking his pants off.

He smiled. She sensed he knew exactly why she'd made the request.

She sat up in bed. She was done letting him run the show. "I'll be back. I need to use the restroom."

When she returned, she got in on the other side of the bed, so that his back was facing her. He started to roll over but she stopped him.

She ran her finger down the middle of his back. Let it dip below the base of his spine.

"Trish," he growled.

"Yes?" she said sweetly.

"What are you—"

"Doing? Why, I'm taking charge."

She pulled on his shoulder so that he lay flat on the bed. Then she straddled him and she was pretty sure his eyes rolled back in his head.

"Go for the grand slam," he said weakly.

AN HOUR LATER, they left the cottage. Trish had her hair up inside the ball cap and wore another ugly shirt, this time a green-and-white stripe, but without the padding. She wore just her own capri pants and they were tight enough that she could stick her gun in the back of her waistband and not have to worry about it falling through. It was damn uncomfortable, however.

Rafe had changed his clothes, too, picking out a tan shirt and pants. He wore the same green fishing hat. He had his gun in his holster and the knife in his boot. He'd grabbed the flashlight at the last minute and she figured that was a good call. If nothing else, knock the hell out of the bad guy.

They both wore sunglasses and took two fishing rods and a tackle box from the Norton shed. As they walked from the cottage to the boat, she was confident that they shouldn't attract undue attention. They looked like any other fashion-challenged couple on the lake. She got in first and Rafe handed her the equipment. As she'd suggested, they took the smaller boat. She knew there was some risk with that. After all, the bad guys might know about Bernie Wilberts's boat and be on the lookout for it. But fortunately, there was nothing too distinctive about it.

They set off at a moderate speed in the middle of the lake. Her nerves were strung tight. She knew this was really their only option. It was hard to fight an enemy when you didn't know who it was. They needed information. Their only lead was the two men that Rafe thought looked suspicious.

Fifteen minutes later she tapped Rafe on the shoulder. "It's just up there a little ways, around the bend in the lake."

"Okay," he said. They were across from a marina larger than the one they'd stopped at earlier. It had multiple places to gas up and there was a row of shops across the street. It looked like a souvenir store, a bar and maybe a small grocery store.

"This is as good a place as any," he added, as he removed his cell phone and battery from his pocket. He snapped the battery in and powered up his phone. He scrolled through the recent calls.

"Anybody?" she asked.

"At least one from everybody on my team. A couple from my boss. Two from blocked numbers."

"What time did they start and stop?"

"First one came in just minutes after I removed the battery. They've continued sporadically since then."

It was just now two o'clock. That meant that Rafe's phone had been dead for about eighteen hours. Not such a long time, really.

But so much had happened. It felt as if it had to be much longer. She watched him scan his contacts and select one. "Who are you dialing?"

"My dentist."

She narrowed her eyes at him, which was a wasted effort because she had on sunglasses. "Suddenly remembered you're due for a cleaning?"

He held up a hand, asking for silence. She heard someone answer on the other line. It was a voice recording. Of course. It was Sunday. The dentist office would not be open. He listened to the whole recording.

Then he disconnected the call and immediately removed the battery. "That will be enough for them to pick up activity," he said.

"What are they going to think if there's activity and you haven't checked in?"

"The worst. Our rule is that if we can, we check in. No exceptions."

She could tell that it bothered him that he'd disregarded a rule that he'd probably helped set. "Maybe you could at least call your boss?"

He shook his head. "I can't. Maybe his phone has been hacked. I just can't take the chance."

The boat was moving fast, the aluminum bottom hitting the water hard. She understood. If they would be able to trace the call back to this area, he would want to get the hell out of there fast.

It was ten minutes later that they saw a boat similar to the one that Rafe had rented slowly cruising the lake. The driver wore a red baseball cap and a white T-shirt. "Is that our relief pitcher?" she asked.

"Relief pitcher, designated hitter, utility guy. Pick your position." Rafe raised his arm and waved.

The boat came closer. And Trish had to remember to shut her mouth. The resemblance was amazing. Of course, there were differences. The man's eyes were just a little rounder, his lower lip just a little less full. But the skin tone was spot-on, he was the same height and weight, and the hair color and cut were perfect.

She could see how if he was coming and going from Rafe's apartment that anyone watching and expecting to see Rafe would think that they had.

The two men nodded to one another. Rafe motioned to her. "Henri, my wife, Trish. Trish, my good friend Henri."

Trish smiled at him. "Thank you for coming."

"What is our plan?" he asked, his German accent quite noticeable.

"Follow us," Rafe said. "We're headed that direction." He motioned toward the far west side of the lake.

When they reached the area that Trish remembered, it was not terribly impressive. There was a relatively narrow channel away from the main body of the lake that quickly broadened into a large circle. Unlike the rest of the lake that was smattered with cottages, docks and boats, this was still undeveloped land. Boaters who ventured into the area probably lost interest relatively quickly—there wasn't much to see except long grass and trees.

Years ago when she and Summer had brought Adie and Keagan to the Ozarks for a few days, they'd gone on a hot air balloon ride. She'd had the chance to see this area from that angle. It had been amazing. The two coves were almost perfect semicircles, a palette of greens contrasting beautifully with the blue water.

In the first cove, there was a boat with two fishermen. Rafe glanced at Trish and she pointed toward the second cove. Ideally, it would be better to have no one else around. That might prove to be impossible but they should try.

The second cove was empty. Trish knew that might be only a temporary reprieve. By the time she dropped Rafe off and returned, hopefully with the men on her tail, one or more boats might have ventured into the area. It wasn't known to be a great fishing spot but the isolation would appeal to some.

She hoped it appealed to the two men, that they didn't smell a trap. If they did, would they just shoot her and be done with it, figuring getting her out of the way was one less body to deal with later?

She voiced none of these concerns. She knew that Rafe was a thread away from shutting down the whole effort, that he was scared for her. She wasn't going to add to that.

She needed to be confident.

Rafe pointed the nose of the boat toward an area at the far side of the cove. There was no sandy shore. The water simply got shallower until it washed up against solid land. He slowed down and motioned for her to get ready to drop the mushroom anchor over the front of the boat. She grasped the nylon rope in her hands, grateful that this wasn't the first time she'd ever done this. Rafe cut the engine and she carefully let out the rope in the waist-high water. The heavy base of the anchor settled into the muddy bottom.

Then Rafe got out of the driver's seat and motioned for her to take his place. She knew what to do. She turned on the engine and slowly backed the boat toward shore. At Rafe's hand signal, she stopped and he was over the rear of the boat, barely making a splash in the water. He waded to shore, pulling the boat after him.

Then he helped her from the boat. It was very quiet, with just a gentle lapping of the water against the land and the occasional squawk of a bird. They did not talk while they waited for Henri to join them.

Once he was there, Rafe led them from the lake, deeper into the tree line. She was grateful for the knee-high fishing boots that she'd borrowed from Mrs. Norton. The grass was long and she worried about snakes. Five minutes later, he stopped.

"This might work." They were the first words he'd said and his voice practically made her jump.

This was a small area that had clearly been someone's campsite at one time. There was a ring of rocks where they'd had a small fire. There was enough space that someone could have pitched a small tent.

He was rubbing his forehead and she wondered if he had a headache. She understood. She had one herself. "I think you're right," she said, hoping she sounded more confident than she felt.

He walked around the perimeter of the cleared space. Every few feet, he would stop and pick up a sturdy-looking stick. When he had an armful, he turned to her. "Remember what I said earlier, that you couldn't get out of the boat? I'm changing my mind. We need to set this up to be believable." He walked over and dumped his load in the fire pit. "If I was right and they were tracking my phone, they will undoubtedly still be in the area of that marina. Once you leave here, go to the grocery store that was across the street. Buy some lighter fluid and matches and maybe some hot dogs and buns. Hell, buy some marshmallows if you want. When you return, come directly to this spot."

He pointed to Henri. "You'll be here. Feeding the fire. Looking unconcerned."

"It's a beautiful day. Why would I be concerned?" Henri asked, his tone light.

Trish knew he understood the risks. Rafe had told her exactly what he'd told Henri before he'd asked the man to participate in their ruse.

"Exactly," Rafe said. He smiled but it didn't reach his eyes.

He still hated this. "Where will you be?" Trish asked.

"Somewhere near, where I can see what's happening."

Where he could manage the situation as best he could. He would protect both her and Henri with his own life.

She really hated this, too.

He turned to her. "You'll need to be vigilant and watch when you pick up a tail. Once that happens, it's straight back here, no more stops, no more delay. I don't think they'll try anything on the open part of the lake. Too many eyes. But once you turn into this cove, they might try to stop you, thinking that they won't run the risk of losing you in the woods."

"What do I do?"

"Do whatever you can to reach land. If they try to apprehend you on the water, you need to use your gun. Once you get on land, I'll be able to protect you, but on the water, I can't be a lot of help to you."

She pressed on her chest because it hurt. "I should go," she said.

"Yeah."

She swallowed hard and started walking. She got five steps before she felt a strong hand on her shoulder. She turned and she was in his arms, as if it was the most natural thing in the world.

"Oh, Trish," he said, his mouth close to her ear. And then he was cupping her face, kissing her. Gently at first. Then more insistent. It reminded her of their last night before he'd disappeared, when they'd made love gently, and then toward morning, he'd taken her again with an urgency that had surprised her.

He kissed her as if he was never going to stop. His

tongue in her mouth, his hands sure and confident as they gripped her. But finally he pulled away and rested his chin against her forehead.

"You won't see me when you get back," he said.

"But you'll be here," she said.

"Yes. Whatever happens, know that I'm here."

"I trust you," she said.

Three little words. Not the three little words that usually made a heart go soft. But in this case, maybe trust was better than love.

"Be safe," he said, his breath coming hard. "Please be safe."

RAFE FOLLOWED TRISH back to the boat and made sure that she got the anchor raised. At the last minute, she took off her striped shirt and her baseball cap and threw them to him.

Then he gave the boat a final push out into deeper water, heard the motor turn over and resisted the overwhelming urge to throw himself into the vessel and wrestle the wheel away from her.

His head hurt. When he moved too quickly the world swam for just a brief second.

Not a good thing if he had to get a shot off quickly.

He wanted to avoid that if at all possible. Truth be told, he, who never ran from any battle, wanted to avoid any altercation. The possibilities of Trish getting hurt were simply too high. He let himself imagine staying on the island with Trish, living off the land, making love a couple of times a day. Of course, that might work in a poorly done movie but in real life it wasn't an option. She had Summer and Adie and Keagan. She had her café.

At one time, she'd had him.

I've moved on.

When he'd made love to her it sure as hell hadn't felt like it. Afterward, for the first time since he'd rescued her from the kitchen chair and she'd backed away from him like a scared animal, he'd felt a little hope.

They couldn't change their history but they could forge a new future. The new guy could get lost. He'd tell him so in no uncertain terms.

But he was jumping the gun. He knew that. Trish was a loving, giving woman but he had perhaps underestimated the pain that she'd endured.

Maybe because that was the only way he could deal with it. Maybe he'd told himself that she'd be sad but that her heart would heal. Maybe he'd been afraid to consider the alternative. That he had dealt her a blow that had knocked her to her knees. Maybe he was doing more of the same right now.

One thing at a time, he told himself. *Concentrate on the most important things. Keeping Trish and Henri safe. Catching the people responsible for all the killing.*

He walked back to the cleared area and found Henri gathering sticks for the fire. "She is very beautiful," Henri said. "She is the one you've been coming to see all these years."

Coming to watch. But there was no need for specifics. "Yes."

"I did not realize that you were married. You surprised me when you said she was your wife."

It had rolled off his tongue pretty easily. It felt right. "We've been estranged," he said.

Henri shook his head. "She does not look at you in that way. She looks with wanting."

Henri might be English-challenged but he had a way with words. Did she want him?

Like for forever?

They hadn't talked about it. There hadn't been much time, really. They'd been together for less than a day after a four-year absence. No wonder things felt strange.

In bed there'd been no strangeness, no awkwardness. He had slid into her body and felt as if he'd finally come home. Peace. There was no other word for it.

But peace rarely lasted and he'd just sent her out as bait. What the hell had he been thinking?

"I don't want her to get hurt," he blurted out.

Henri shrugged. "Then we'll have to work very hard to make sure she isn't."

Chapter Seventeen

As she drove the boat across the lake, Trish was overly conscious of her hair flying in the wind. After all, it was her blue-light special signal. *Red-haired woman here. Come and get me!*

She tied up at the marina and wiped her sweaty hands on the edge of her shirt. When she crossed the street, she made it a point to look both ways twice. Not because she was worried about the traffic, but because it gave her a chance to look around. She did not see two middle-aged men like Rafe had described.

She knew that did not mean they weren't there.

She opened the door of the small grocery store and almost sighed when the cool air hit her. It was another hot afternoon in Missouri. It dawned on her that just a day ago when she'd bought groceries, her biggest concern had been getting them home before they got hot. Now it was getting them back to Rafe before she got shot.

Hot, shot or worse. Taken. Funny how that could be worse than getting shot and dying. But the hours she'd spent yesterday with Big Tony and Anthony had been horrible. She'd felt so vulnerable. She didn't ever want to feel that way again.

And if she was taken, she knew Rafe would do whatever it took to get her back safely. Even if he died in the process.

Better to just get it over with with a bullet to the brain.

Not that she was hoping for either alternative. What she really wanted was to buy her few groceries, get in her boat, have the men follow her back to the island and then let Rafe deal with them on his terms.

And she'd just stand off to the side and watch.

She wasn't cut out for this kind of stuff. And up until yesterday, she'd never imagined that Rafe was, either. But she was learning about this man that she'd married.

He'd figured out a way to fool everyone who was tracking his movements from Italy to the United States. Then he'd found her at the cottage and disabled both Big Tony and Anthony to free her. And that was basically nothing compared to what he'd done after the cottage had exploded. After nearly drowning, he'd managed to get both of them back in the boat, across the lake and into the Norton cottage. With a head injury.

He was amazing, really.

Now, likely with a concussion, he was getting ready to confront the enemy. All she had to do was lead them there.

She wandered up and down the aisles of the small store. There were only four with a small freezer section across the back wall. As Rafe had suggested, she picked up a package of hot dogs and buns. She skipped the marshmallows, thinking something that sweet would make her sick for sure. She bought two bottles of water. No telling how long this might last and she didn't want either of them getting dehydrated.

And because the potato chips that she'd bought the day before had been scattered from here to wherever by the blast, she added a bag of those. Comfort food in an uncomfortable situation.

She took her merchandise up to the cash register and waited behind two women both dressed in swimsuits with cover-ups thrown over them. They had on cute sandals that made her very conscious of the tall rubber boots that she wore. She felt clumsy and out of place.

All the better to attract attention, she told herself. Which, she realized, was exactly what she'd done when she shifted to pull money out of her pocket and saw a dark-haired man in the corner of the store. Watching her.

Her twenty-dollar bill fluttered down onto the checkout lane. "Sorry," she mumbled.

The clerk smiled and picked up the money. Then she bagged Trish's groceries and gave her the change. Trish stuffed it back in her pocket, telling herself to breathe, just breathe.

She looped the plastic sack over her wrist, keeping her hands free. Then she walked out of the store, looking twice each direction before she crossed the road again.

She forced herself to walk, not run, down the long dock. Then she was in the boat, untying the ropes, tossing them on the floor of the boat. She started the motor and pulled away. Slowly. A careful boater.

Certainly not a woman whose heart was about to jump out of her chest. She did not look behind her. But she listened for the sound of another engine.

And she was pretty sure she heard one.

RAFE HAD CHOSEN his spot carefully. He was uphill from the clearing. He could see both the lake and Henri. When he heard Trish's boat, he took in three very deep breaths to settle his nerves.

She dropped her anchor close to shore, got out of the boat with plastic bags on her arm and sloshed through the water to the shore.

She waved to Henri and he waved back. Then she showed him what she'd bought. When she pulled a magazine out of her sack and tossed it in his lap, he realized that she was brilliant.

She needed to give them an excuse for not talking. That excuse was this week's *People* magazine.

Henri caught on and started flipping pages. Trish sat next to him and got busy putting hot dogs on the ends of sharp sticks that Henri had placed near the fire.

Nice day for a picnic.

They were playing it perfectly.

And he thought it might be for naught when he didn't see another boat follow her into the cove. And after about ten minutes, he was just about to call it a good effort, when out of the corner of his eye, he saw movement onshore.

The two men that he'd seen that morning were furtively walking along the shore. They each had a gun in hand.

They must have thought it was too dangerous to bring their boat into the cove. They had probably left it just around the edge, in the main part of the lake.

He saw the exact moment that they saw Henri and Trish. They stopped in their tracks, looked at one another and nodded. He got ready. If they raised their guns, he was going to have to take them out.

But they didn't. He wasn't that surprised. He thought they might attempt to take him alive. All the better so that he could be tortured later.

He waited for them to split up, so that one could approach from behind.

But they did nothing. Except the man in the lead pulled out a cell phone and appeared to be sending a text. Did they really need instructions? Or permission? Who the hell was pulling the strings in this operation?

Meanwhile, Trish had cooked two hot dogs, put each one inside a bun and handed one to Henri. They were eating and Henri was looking through his magazine, his head bent down.

Rafe wanted to rush the men and demand answers. But he waited.

Twenty-seven minutes and forty-two seconds later, his patience was rewarded.

And then sorely tested because something was happening but he wasn't exactly sure what. The man with the phone had quickly pulled it out of his pocket, looked at the screen and then nodded, as if satisfied. Then he pointed to his partner to circle around behind the clearing.

Rafe followed the man who was moving. As he did so, he heard the engine of a boat. He looked over his shoulder. He still had a clear view of the lake but the boat was out too far for him to clearly see the person at the wheel.

But he didn't doubt for one minute that it had something to do with the information that had come across the man's phone.

The boat was drawing closer. Henri and Trish had to hear it but they were continuing to act unconcerned. Trish had relaxed back on the sand, as if her primary goal in life was to catch some rays on her face.

It humbled him that she trusted him to figure out a way to save them all.

He hoped to hell it wasn't misplaced.

TRISH STRETCHED BACK, her upper body propped up by digging her elbows in the sand. She kept swallowing because otherwise she thought she might vomit her recently eaten hot dog. What the hell was happening? It was taking forever. She wanted to know what Rafe was thinking, what he was doing.

I'll be there. It had been his promise. She would not doubt him.

But when she heard the engine of the boat, she wanted to leap up from the sand and call out to him, to warn him. But instead, she closed her eyes and lifted her face to the sun.

She knew something was wrong when Henri, who had been humming softly under his breath, stopped. She opened her eyes just as two men emerged from the trees with guns in their hands.

Chapter Eighteen

One was the man that Rafe had described. Midforties, brown hair, dressed in brand-new clothes. The other was much older, balding, with more gray than brown in his hair. He wore a linen shirt and what looked to be silk trousers. They were wet up to the knees where he'd waded to shore.

Henri tossed his magazine aside and had stood up. He stepped in front of Trish, as if protecting her.

"Search them," the older man snarled.

Forties Guy did. All he found was a pack of gum in Henri's pocket.

"I prefer to meet in my home, in civilized conditions," the older man said, his tone condescending. "But your actions, Mr. Roper, rendered that impossible. Or should I call you Ryan Weber? That is, after all, what my sons knew you as."

Luciano Maladucci. It had to be. He had a soft Italian accent.

Henri said nothing. She knew that he was going to avoid talking as long as possible.

Maladucci stepped closer, close enough now that Trish could smell the expensive cologne that he'd evidently bathed in. With his free hand, he batted away a bug from his neck.

Then he clamped that same hand on her biceps and roughly yanked her toward him. Henri made a move to pull her back but Forties Guy stepped forward with his gun pointed at Henri's heart.

"I'm dreadfully sorry to interrupt your picnic," Maladucci said, "but your husband has caused me a great deal of trouble and I simply can't allow it. He needs to understand the consequences of his continued interest in my family. It means I will have an interest in *his* family."

Rafe had been right.

Where the hell was Rafe?

Waving his gun in the direction of the lake, Maladucci said, "In my country, little boys are taught to fish before they can walk."

Huh?

"Knowing how to scale a fish is a useful skill," he added. With his thumb, he lifted up the edge of his expensive shirt and put his gun back into the small leather holster that he wore on his hip. Then he pulled a knife.

Long, shiny, maybe a ten-inch blade, slightly curved.

And he put it up to her throat.

But he looked at Henri. "You're going to watch her die. And know how I feel every day when I think about my sons rotting in that prison. I have waited a long time for this," he said. "Too long. Demí said that it wasn't worth it. The risk was too great. But he's wrong. It is absolutely worth it."

He grabbed a big swath of her hair, knotting it up in his fist. "This is very pretty," he said, his voice almost purring. "I'll bet you like it," he said, again looking at Henri.

No response from Henri. That seemed to agitate Mala-

ducci even more. "You are not much of a man if you will
not defend those that you love," he said. Then he swung
his knife toward her and the sharp blade connected, just
above his clenched fist, and a foot of hair floated to the
ground.

Her heart was thudding in her chest. Not over the
loss of some hair. But that knife was very sharp and he
seemed to know how to use it.

It had stunned Henri. He was white-faced and was
looking from side to side.

Maladucci noticed. "There's no one coming," he said.
He pointed toward Forties Guy. "I sent his partner up onto
the hill where he'd have a clear view of the lake so that
he could make sure that we're not interrupted."

Maladucci tilted his head back. "Monty," he called
out. "Are we still alone?"

There was silence. Maladucci looked at Forties Guy,
who shrugged.

"Monty?" Maladucci called out.

When there was no answer, he pointed to Forties Guy.
"Go find him," he said.

She turned her head to watch Forties Guy climb the
hill but soon lost him in the trees. She heard him crash-
ing through the brush.

Then there was nothing.

"Jacques?" Maladucci yelled.

Jacques didn't answer.

Maladucci moved faster than she would have anticipated. He wrapped his arm around her throat and the
knife came frighteningly close to cutting her carotid ar-
tery. She did not move.

"What the hell is going on?" he demanded.

Henri shrugged.

"Why the hell don't you say something, you bastard," Maladucci yelled, sounding insane. He tightened his grip on her neck, cutting off her air. She started grabbing at his arm and quickly realized that he was too strong.

It was now or never. She clenched her fist and jammed her elbow back. She heard a pop and he sagged behind her, almost taking her down with him.

She scrambled away. Oh, God. Had she pushed a rib into his lung? Had she seriously injured him? It wasn't until she looked at him that she realized he had a bullet hole in his forehead. And Rafe was running down the hill like a high school track star.

"Get away," he yelled.

She couldn't. Her legs had given out on her. She sagged into the sand. "He's dead," she said.

Rafe didn't even break stride. He got close, checked for a pulse and, only then, turned to her. "Oh my God, Trish. Are you okay?" he asked.

Before she could answer, he bent to the ground and picked up the pile of hair. "Your hair. Your beautiful hair."

"I needed a trim," she said and grimaced when her own voice trembled. She needed to be strong. He certainly had been. "The other men. Monty and Jacques?" she asked, her voice stronger.

"Incapacitated. Not dead."

"That was close, man," Henri said, regaining some of his aplomb.

"Now what?" she asked.

Rafe was already pulling out his phone. "We call the police. You'll both need to give statements. I'll call my boss, let him know what's going on. We'll have to move on arresting his older son for his involvement in the biological warfare."

"It's really over," she said. "I can go home."

"Yes."

She didn't want to have this conversation with Henri listening in. But she needed to know. "Are you coming back to Ravesville, Rafe?" she asked, as casually as she could when her heart was racing in her chest.

"Do you want me to?" he asked.

"I think we have things to talk about," she said.

He drew in a deep breath. "We'll talk," he said.

Chapter Nineteen

Summer cried when she walked in the door. Just like she had every time she'd seen Trish for the past week. She hugged her so hard that Trish was confident she'd bruised a rib.

"You know, with your hair shorter, we look more alike than ever," Summer said.

True. Summer had worn her hair shoulder-length for years. After Trish's stylist had evened out her hair, it was just a few inches longer.

Plenty left for Rafe to wrap his hands in.

Except that Rafe was MIA. Well, not really missing. She knew where he was. He'd had to return to DC to meet with his boss shortly after he'd taken care of pesky little details like getting people arrested and transported to the appropriate place.

It had been a little hard to piece the puzzle together with Luciano Maladucci dead. But there was a ballistics match to Jacques' gun for M.A. and for Mrs. Wilberts. The hits had been ordered by Maladucci, or so Jacques said, and there was little reason to disbelieve him.

Both Jacques and Monty had denied any involvement in Milo's death and Trish had been inclined to believe them. She would always believe that it had been Maladucci. He was good with a knife and he seemed the type to gloat over a dying man, which had probably prompted Milo's deathbed warning.

The part that didn't make sense was the rocket launcher to the cottage, killing the Paradinis and Bernie Wilberts. Again, Jacques and Monty denied involvement, said that they'd arrived at the lake the following morning after being summoned by Luciano Maladucci in the middle of the night.

Maybe it had been Maladucci and he'd got Bernie Wilberts confused with Rafe. If so, he'd no doubt been very angry when the police identified Bernie as the victim based on his license plate. But that didn't really make sense because Maladucci wouldn't have expected Rafe to even be in the States at the time of the explosion. He was supposedly still in the air, on his way from Italy. In the end, she supposed it didn't matter. Knowing the truth wouldn't bring them back. The cops had found some text messages on Bernie Wilberts's phone that showed he was a bad guy. They'd told her that he sold a bunch of drugs, the kind that were killing teens.

And it was hard to be sympathetic about the Paradinis. They had planned to kill her. They had killed Duke.

She was grateful to the Hollister brothers, who had helped her look for Duke's remains. They'd been unsuccessful in finding them, and because hope really did spring eternal, she'd stapled his picture on every fence post and fishing pier in the area, just in case.

But there'd been no word and it had been a week.

"When's Rafe coming home?" Summer asked.

"I'm not sure. We had almost no time to talk before he had to return to DC."

Summer lowered her voice, obviously cognizant that

her handsome husband was in the kitchen, getting them tea. "Are you going to be okay, Trish?"

"I don't know," she said. "Things are no more settled then they were when he walked into the kitchen and I fainted dead away."

"Don't say the word *dead*," Summer said. She wasn't teasing.

She was right. Too many dead people. And Milo's funeral was tomorrow. Rafe had sent an email, promising that he'd be back. She'd tried his phone and got his voice mail.

They'd sort of connected. Kind of like they were sort of married.

"Rafe will make it," Summer said, as if she'd been reading her mind. Having a twin was really scary sometimes.

"I'm sure he'll do his best," Trish said. Her voice sounded tight and pinched and she knew that Summer heard it.

"Give him a chance," Summer said. "I saw the way he looked at you before he left. He loves you."

And she loved him. Always had. Always would.

But was it enough? He'd deceived her. For what he'd thought were good reasons, but the four years of pain she'd endured could not be so easily forgotten.

"We're planning to talk," Trish said. It was all she was willing to commit to. "Now, let's make sure we've got things covered tomorrow."

An hour later, she left Summer's house and went by the café. They'd stayed closed the entire week. They would re-open on Monday, the day after tomorrow. Food and paper products had been delivered yesterday. She'd shoved the refrigerated items into the cooler but had left the boxes of canned goods in their boxes. She needed to get those unpacked and on the shelves. It wouldn't hurt to cut up some vegetables for soup, either.

An hour later, things were looking pretty good when her cell phone buzzed. She pulled it out and her pulse kicked up. Rafe was twenty minutes out.

WHEN SHE MET him at the door of the café, she leaned forward for a chaste kiss on the cheek. So, that was the way it was, huh?

No way. He'd had some time to think this week. He was coming back to Ravesville and they were going to have the life that they'd started four years ago.

"How are you?" he asked.

"Fine. Come in," she said, stepping aside.

It felt weird, her treating him like a guest. He wanted to grab her and kiss the hell out of her but knew that wasn't what she had in mind when he took a stool at the counter and she walked behind it.

She looked tired. But good. "I like the hair," he said.

"Thanks," she said as she took a seat beside him. "I may keep it this length. I mean, I know you liked it long, liked to…" Her hands fluttered at her sides.

She was nervous. He'd been gone too long and they hadn't had time to talk before he'd left.

But there had been a lot to handle. The first thing he'd done while he, Trish and Henri were still in the cove was call his boss. When he'd given him a rundown of everything that had happened since he'd abruptly left Italy, there'd been long periods of silence on the phone. Rafe knew the man was surprised and probably trying to figure how best to proceed.

It had taken a week but now he had good news to share

with Trish, news that should quiet her nerves. "Mario Maladucci and a host of others have been arrested. There are a myriad of charges, the most serious dealing with conspiracy and intent to commit a terrorist act on American soil."

"It's over? Really over."

"It is," he said.

The silence stretched. He ran his index finger along the edge of the counter. Back and forth.

She watched him. "We had that custom-made," she said. It was easier to talk about counters than the things that really mattered.

He nodded. "I know. I remember the day they delivered it. You were so excited."

She stood up, very straight. "You'd been gone for over a year when the counter was delivered."

He stilled his hand. There could be no more lies. "I told you that Henri would take my place when I needed to get away."

"Yes."

"I would come here. I rented the apartment on the second floor of the building across the street."

"What?" She was blinking her eyes fast.

He swallowed hard. "Sometimes I just needed to be close," he said.

The color drained from her face as she sat again. "Are you telling me, Rafe Roper, that you *watched* me?"

He would tell her all of it. "Yes. More than once. I was in your house, too, when you weren't home."

She stood up, her motions awkward. "My heart was breaking and you had the capacity to make it better. All you had to do was walk across the street. Or wait for me to come home one night. My God, Rafe. Why didn't you do that?"

"I couldn't."

"Yes. You could have," she said. "You could have told me the truth and let me make the decision. Instead, you made it for me."

He was losing her. He could tell. "But you, you were always talking, laughing. You seemed happy. How the hell was I supposed to know?"

She opened her mouth, then shut it. She turned and started to walk away.

"Trish," he said. They had come through so much. How could he lose her now? "Where are you going?"

She turned, just halfway. "I…I can't be with—"

She stopped. Her cell phone was buzzing. She fished it out of her purse and read the screen.

"Trish," he said. He was not above begging.

"I have a date tonight," she said, sounding almost dazed. "That's where I'm going. On. My. Date."

"No," he said.

She stared at him. "You lost the right to tell me what to do a long time ago."

She took three more steps, turned the door handle and walked out the back door of the café to where her new Jeep was parked.

TRISH WALKED THROUGH the empty rooms of her house, touching nothing. The space felt huge.

She would sell the place. Should have done it years ago. What would Rafe have thought when he sneaked into town and saw the big For Sale sign?

You were always talking, laughing. Had she been so convincing that he was fooled? Surely Milo would have told him? But to be fair, she never let Milo see more than a little of her despair. She'd always figured the poor man had his own problems—he didn't need to shoulder hers, too.

Maybe if Milo had gone to Rafe and said, *Hey, buddy, she's falling apart.* Maybe that would have made the difference?

She'd been so angry with Rafe. When her cell phone had buzzed, she'd almost ignored it. But then had realized it might be about Duke. Maybe someone had found him. When she'd seen the text, it had jolted her back into the reality of her life.

She'd intended to cancel the stupid date but had forgotten to do so. But just that quick, she'd been grateful that she hadn't. She needed to think of something else besides Rafe's duplicity. She'd be poor company tonight but she would meet Barry North and they would have dinner. She would pay for her own. Heck, she'd buy his, too, just for the principle of it.

Then she'd tell him that she wasn't interested in a second date. Because even if she couldn't ever forgive Rafe, she also couldn't imagine ever loving anyone else.

She stopped walking when she got to her bedroom. After dressing in a black skirt and a sleeveless white silky blouse, she caught a glimpse of herself in the mirror. Her skin had actually tanned while she was in the Ozarks.

A visible change.

So many more beneath the surface.

She pulled her long hair into a ponytail and then wrapped it tight into a bun at the nape of her neck. She slipped her feet into black sandals with delicate gold buckles.

She drove to Hamerton and found the restaurant. She checked her watch. She was twenty minutes early.

It gave her too much time to think. What was Rafe doing right now? What was he thinking? Was he tying up the loose ends of his investigation so that he could leave after Milo's funeral?

She pressed a hand against her stomach, knowing that the sudden pain was not from hunger but something much more elemental. Love. Loss.

Indecision.

She pulled out her cell phone, thought about calling him. Couldn't. She wasn't ready to talk to him yet. Instead, she sent a quick text to Summer. At Mulder's in Hamerton. Date with Barry North from Kansas City. Ever since her lake experience, she'd felt the need to check in more frequently, to make sure that somebody else had key information.

She turned her phone to Silent. That was enough for now. Summer would have a thousand questions and she didn't want to answer them just yet.

At ten minutes before seven, she opened the heavy front door of Mulder's. The foyer was dimly lit with sconces on the wall. There was a woman, dressed all in black, her arms wrapped around several menus. Before Trish could give her name, a man approached from the dining room.

"Trish?" he asked, his voice tentative.

"Yes," she said, her voice higher than usual. She was nervous.

"I recognized you from your picture," he said, smiling.

She extended her hand. His online picture had been of him skiing down some mountain. Up close, he was a good-looking guy. He was probably midforties with an athletic build and a full head of hair.

If she'd been looking, he would have warranted a second glance. She was going to have to make sure that he understood that it was her, not him, that precluded a second date.

"I was just about to walk out to my car," he said.

She glanced at her watch. "Was I late?" she asked.

"I just realized that I forgot my billfold out there."

She started to tell him that he wouldn't need it, that she intended to cover dinner. But she didn't want to have that conversation now, before they'd even ordered drinks.

"You can wait here or you're welcome to walk with me," he said. "It's a beautiful night."

It was. It was still light outside and they were on the main street of Hamerton. It was safe. Trish smiled at the hostess. "We'll be right back."

He held the door for her. "That way," he said, pointing a finger.

They passed her new Jeep and got to the end of the block. He turned right. "Just got my car painted," he said. "Didn't want to park too close to anyone else."

The side street was much quieter than the main street and she felt suddenly uncomfortable. Maybe her experience at the lake had made her hypersensitive but she wasn't ignoring her gut. "You know, I just forgot that I need to make a phone call," Trish said. She started to turn. "I think I'll head back to the restaurant and do that—"

He yanked on her arm, pulling her into a dark doorway. His hand was over her mouth before she could scream.

"Sh-sh-shut up," he said, his mouth very close to her ear. "Shut up or I'll k-k-kill you here."

RAFE HAD LEFT the café and had gone to the only other place that he felt comfortable—the empty apartment across the street. He prowled around the space. The idea of Trish going on a date with another man ate at him, making him want to lash out at someone.

He needed to do something productive.

Hell, maybe he'd mow Trish's grass. It had rained several times this past week and the grass had to be growing like crazy.

He drove to Trish's house and let himself in with the key that he'd always had. He supposed that she'd want it back.

He wandered around the empty house, knowing that he was stalling. If he didn't start the yard soon, it would get dark before he got it finished.

He made one more pass through the house. He could smell her perfume in her bedroom and he clenched his fist thinking of another man sniffing at her damn neck. And at all the other places where he knew she liked to dabble a little scent.

He saw Trish's computer on the desk. She'd never said how she'd met her date. Had it been online? The guy could be a major creep.

Or he might be a really nice guy that she liked.

Which one was he more afraid of?

He ran his finger along the edge of the computer as he sat down at the desk. Would she think he was out of line? He hesitated for just one more second.

He'd rather be out of line than lose her to some other guy. He flipped open the lid. Fortunately, there was no password. He opened the internet browser and went right for the tab that appeared to be for the online dating website. A click, a simple click, and he would have information on Trish's date.

He stopped. She was already so angry with him. Would this push her over the edge?

He closed the computer, pushed his chair back. Rubbed the back of his neck. Christ, he was tired.

He stood, pulling his keys out of his pocket. He'd mow the grass tomorrow, before Milo's funeral. He hadn't given Trish the privacy she deserved before. He sure as hell could now.

He had his hand on the doorknob.

Aw, hell.

In six steps he was back at the desk and within seconds he had the computer open. He clicked on the right tab.

And his damn head about exploded.

He'd recognize that profile anywhere. The ski jacket added a little bulk and the stocking cap hid the high forehead.

But it was his boss.

Kevin Leonard.

There was no good reason for him to be dating Trish.

But a slew of bad reasons. And each one of them had something to do with what had happened at the lake.

He picked up Trish's landline phone and quickly dialed. Summer answered on the second ring. "What is going on, sis?" she asked. "I just got your text and—"

"It's Rafe," he said. "I'm at Trish's house. She sent you a text? Where is she?" he asked.

"Why?" she said, her tone more guarded.

"Listen, Summer. I don't have time to explain. But I think she's in trouble."

"In Hamerton. At Mulder's. Oh, Rafe—"

"Don't worry," he said, interrupting her. "I'll find her. And when I do, I'm never letting her out of my sight again."

BARRY NORTH HAD hit her hard in the stomach, then stuffed her in the trunk of his car while she was trying to catch her breath. It was dark and hot and she felt as if she was going to throw up. She'd found the emergency trunk release and realized that it was somehow disconnected.

This hadn't been a spur-of-the-moment decision.

He'd planned this. He'd led her down the side street on purpose. He'd lied about his car being just painted. When he'd put her in the trunk, she'd seen the heavy white dust on the black car.

Think. Think, she told herself. What else had he said? *Shut up or I'll kill you here.*

Horrible, horrible words. He'd stuttered when he'd said them.

Hadn't she just heard about someone who stuttered when they were nervous? *Oh my God.* It had been Rafe's boss, Kevin Leonard. What else had Rafe said about him? All she could remember was that his shoes were always shined.

She breathed in hot air and told herself to think. Why would Rafe's boss have struck up an online relationship with her? Why would he stuff her in the trunk of a car?

There could be only one explanation. Rafe had been right all along. He'd been concerned that it was someone on his own team that might be trying to kill them. It was the person leading the team.

The only reasonable explanation was that Kevin Leonard was working with the Maladuccis. But they'd been arrested. Why keep going?

But not all of them had been arrested. Not the younger son. What was his name?

Demí. That was right. When Luciano Maladucci had held the knife up to her throat and talked about getting revenge against Rafe, he'd said that Demí had said it wasn't worth it, that the risk was too much.

In everything that had happened, she'd forgotten to

tell Rafe that and he hadn't heard it himself because he'd been too far away.

But the younger son had to be a part of this. Was Kevin Leonard somehow in cahoots with Demí?

It was more than she could fathom. But she needed to wrap her head around it. She also needed to pay attention to everything else. She needed to keep track of how long they drove so that she could estimate the miles once they stopped. Were there other sounds? Trains? Car horns? Anything that would give her an idea.

They were going fast, which told her that they'd left the city limits of Hamerton. She let out a small scream when he turned hard and she slid to the side, knocking her shoulder into the side of the trunk.

She'd been such a fool. But she'd been so intent on teaching Rafe some kind of lesson.

Rafe. Oh, God. She loved him so much and she was never going to get the chance to tell him.

The car stopped suddenly and she prepared herself to come out swinging, scratching, screaming. Whatever it took. She wasn't going to make it easy for this guy.

She heard his door open then shut. Then nothing.

Seconds turned into a full minute.

Was he simply going to leave her here? To die a slow death in a hot trunk.

It was crazy.

And as much as she didn't want to face the man, she didn't want to die alone.

She started to scream.

RAFE MADE THE twenty-minute drive to Hamerton in twelve minutes. He pulled into an empty parking spot and was out of the car and opening the restaurant door in seconds.

He stepped across the small foyer and into the dining room. He scanned the tables.

Damn. She wasn't there. Had Summer been wrong?

Trish would not have lied to her about it. There would be no reason to. He turned to see a young woman, walking at a leisurely pace. "Sir?" she asked. "Table for one?"

"I'm looking for a woman, long red hair, with a man, midforties, brown hair."

She glanced around the room. He resisted the urge to get in her face in an attempt to hurry her.

"She would have arrived about fifteen minutes ago," he said.

The woman's blue eyes opened a little wider. "There was a woman, really pretty, who had red hair. I'm not sure how long it was. It was in a really cute bun."

"Where is she?"

"The gentleman that she was with forgot his wallet in his car. They went to get it. She said she'd be right back but that didn't happen. I just gave their table away."

"What direction?" he asked. "What direction did they turn when they left?"

She shrugged. "I think to the right."

He started running. Saw her car and searched it quickly. It was empty. When he got to the end of the block, he debated whether he should turn left and cross the street or turn right.

He thought about his boss. Conservative Kevin. Suit always pressed. Silk tie. Hair always trimmed.

He turned right.

And ran, stopping just long enough to look in every parked car. He got all the way to the end of the block. In Washington, DC, Kevin drove a Toyota Camry. But he'd have rented a car here. It was like looking for a needle in a haystack.

He ran his hand through his hair. Tilted his head back. And saw the man.

Second-floor window. Sitting in his chair. Watching the street.

Rafe crossed the street, stood underneath the window. He waved his arm. "Hey, sir," he yelled. "I'm looking for a woman, red hair, in a bun. Have you seen her?"

The old man stood. He was wearing pajamas. "I already called the police," he said, his Southern drawl heavy.

"What? Why?"

"Because where I come from, young man, you don't hit your woman and lock her in the trunk."

TRISH STOPPED SCREAMING when she started choking on her dry throat. No one was coming. No one was going to help her.

The man hadn't told her to be quiet, hadn't threatened her. That told her one thing. She was in the middle of nowhere.

How long did it take to die of thirst in a hot car?

A day? Two at the most. It wouldn't be an easy death.

But she couldn't simply give up. Summer knew that she'd gone on the date. She'd be expecting to hear from her in a couple of hours. When that didn't happen, she'd summon help.

Rafe would look, too. He'd been full-time busy saving her life this past week.

He would not stop until he found her. *Please, please, let him be in time.*

RAFE PACED THE SIDEWALK, waiting for the police. The man in the pajamas had come downstairs and was standing on his porch. But he wasn't talking. *I'll tell my story to law enforcement.* That was what he'd said when Rafe had demanded to know more about the man, the car, the direction they'd gone. Rafe had pulled his badge. "I'm a federal agent," he'd said.

The man just shook his head. He wasn't impressed.

Right now Rafe wasn't all that impressed with being a federal agent. Not when his boss could do something like this.

He'd thought about pulling his gun and forcing the old guy to talk but knew that was only going to ultimately delay him. He might need the local police.

He used his time to call Chase Hollister. When the man answered, Rafe quickly filled him in. "It's Rafe Roper. I think Trish has been kidnapped by my boss, Kevin Leonard, outside Mulder's restaurant in Hamerton."

"Got it," Chase said, knowing better than to waste time with stupid questions. "We're on our way. Stay in touch."

Next he called Daniel, who had hung around Ravesville all week. He was intending to go back to Chicago after Milo's funeral. Rafe wanted all the help he could get.

He'd just finished his conversation with Daniel when he heard the sounds of approaching sirens. Two squad cars pulled up. A male officer in one, a female officer in the other. Probably everybody on duty on a quiet night in Hamerton, Missouri.

He kept his identification in his hand. Maybe they'd be more impressed.

"I'm Officer Wagner and this is Officer Billet," said the male officer when they got close. "Which one of you made the call?"

Wagner and Billet were both in their thirties and he suspected they had several years of experience, based on the quiet confidence of their approach. But he doubted they'd ever come up against anyone like Kevin Leonard before. The man was exceptionally smart. That was something Rafe had always admired about him.

Rafe stepped forward. "I'm Rafe Roper and I'm a federal agent." He held out his badge for them to examine. "This man saw a woman get assaulted and pushed into the trunk of a car. My..." He stopped. It might do more harm than good to identify Trish as his wife. They would doubt that he could be impartial.

They would be right.

"The woman is Trish Wright, a witness in my protection. The driver of the car is Kevin Leonard, also a federal agent."

The two officers looked at each other. Officer Billet recovered first. She stepped forward and addressed the old man. "What's your name and what did you see?"

"My name is Walter Wilson and I saw these two people—a couple, I thought. Not walking hand in hand but chatting, like they knew each other. Then, all of a sudden—" his voice lowered, as if he was enjoying the storytelling "—the man yanked her into that doorway, right there, and then he hit her. Like he was going for middleweight champion of the world."

Rafe was going to rip Leonard apart.

"Then when she was bent double, trying to catch her breath, he popped his trunk open and pushed her inside. Then he took off."

She was injured. No doubt scared to death. He'd been so damn stupid to be satisfied with catching Luciano and Mario Maladucci. His gut had told him that it went deeper.

A few things made sense now.

The reluctance that Kevin Leonard had had about Rafe coming back on his team four years ago. The feeling that the Maladuccis were sometimes a step ahead of them. And most recently, that first phone call to his boss. Kevin had seemed shocked at the news he was telling him. He hadn't been shocked by that. He'd been shocked to hear from Rafe because he knew that Maladucci intended to kill him.

"What kind of car?" Rafe demanded.

Both of the cops gave him a dirty look.

"We're wasting time," he said.

The old man held up his hand. "He was driving one of them new Cadillacs. A nice black one. Shame to let a car like that get so dirty. Lots of white dust. If I had to guess, it's spent some time parked near the quarry."

Rafe knew the quarry. He'd spent a year working in Hamerton, building the new mall. They had got cement from the quarry. It was almost straight east, just a few miles outside of Ravesville.

It would help considerably to have an area to start. But dust could blow some distance and that meant there would still be multiple country roads, with multiple houses and outbuildings to search. It would take time. Time that Trish might not have. "Listen to me," he said. "He'll be armed and dangerous. I have backup coming. Chief Hollister from Ravesville."

"We know Chase Hollister," Officer Wagner said.

"Good," Rafe said, already running for his car. "Communicate with me through him," he said, over his shoulder. "He's got my number."

Rafe got into his car and headed east, driving ninety on roads meant for fifty-five.

He was going to be too late. He could feel it in his gut.

RAFE WAS GOING to be too late. That was her first thought when the trunk lid suddenly popped open and she saw *her date* standing there, now holding a hacksaw.

He motioned for her to get out of the trunk and she saw that he also had a gun.

She didn't want to get any closer to the saw or the gun but there was absolutely no chance of running away if she didn't get out. She summoned every bit of courage that she had and threw a leg over the side. Soon she was standing next to the vehicle. Her legs were not steady and she tried to calm herself by taking a few quick deep breaths.

She glanced down and knew she was right about the identity of her captor. The car might be filthy but her date was neatly dressed and his shoes were super shiny. "So, Barry," she said, "or should I just call you Kevin?"

He reared back in surprise. "W-w-well," he said. He drew in a deep breath as if he, too, needed to settle his nerves. "I guess the need for introductions is over."

"Why are you doing this?"

He didn't answer. Just looked at her.

It didn't matter why. What mattered was getting away. She'd been right. The area was deserted. It felt a bit like the end of the earth. The gravel road dwindled away into patches of dirt and grass just twenty yards past the one-story white bungalow that had probably been new in the '40s and got its last coat of paint in 1970. There were no screens on the windows and several of the panes were cracked. There was no yard, just an accumulation of crabgrass and weeds.

She was not going in that house. He'd have to kill her outside.

"That's going to be messy," she said, looking at the saw, buying time. "Based on what you told me in your emails, I thought you were the orderly sort. You know, clean kitchen counters and such."

"It's not for me," he said.

She looked around. "I'm not sure that squirrel in the tree has the strength to use it."

He smiled, showing even, white teeth. "You're quite funny. I noticed that in your emails. It's no wonder Rafe Wonder likes you."

Rafe *Wonder*. Was that another one of his aliases?

Kevin Leonard laughed. "That's what I call him. Rafe Wonder. Because he's a damn Wonder Boy. Always getting it right. Tenacious. Patriotic to a fault. Guess that's good when you're in a position to be having Sunday dinners at the White House with your old college roommate and his father."

He was jealous of Rafe. Was that what this was about? It had to be more.

He looked at his watch and scowled. This had to be about the person he was expecting. The person the saw was for.

"I would think you'd be happy," she said. "After all, isn't Rafe catching Luciano Maladucci a feather in your cap? After all, you lead the team."

"The agency pays me a pittance," he said. "If you want to get rich, don't work for the government."

"So instead, you work for the Maladuccis," she said.

He looked at the saw with distaste. "This wouldn't be necessary if you and Rafe had died at the cottage the way you were supposed to."

"You launched that rocket," she said. It was the only thing that made sense.

"Yes. When Rafe called to tell me that he'd left the surveillance site because he was ill, I knew he was lying. Rafe would have stuck it out, you know, country before self. There was a reason he left and it had to be a good one. I thought it was possible that he'd gotten word about Milo and his unfortunate demise."

"You did that," she accused. She had not thought it was possible to hate the man more.

He shook his head. "That was Luciano's handiwork. It was humorous, really. Rafe was watching Maladucci's house and the man was already in the United States, had already killed Milo. Anyway, it gnawed at me that Rafe had left a trail that we could so easily follow. Buying the charter flight ticket, renting the car. He was usually much sharper in the field. And I just knew that, somehow, Rafe had managed to leave Italy earlier than we thought. I followed that hunch to Heelie Lake and some lovely young woman with way too many tattoos confirmed that hours earlier a handsome guy driving a BMW had been inquiring about a woman with long red hair. I drove to the cottage, saw the black BMW and thought it was my chance to end it all. The Paradinis, you, Rafe. Everyone dead. Maladucci would have thought I was brilliant to tie things up so neatly."

"You must have been really upset when that plan didn't come together," she said.

"Sh-sh-shut up," he said. He looked down the gravel road.

"Don't you hate it when people aren't on time?" she said, turning slightly, trying to get a better angle to see if he'd left the keys in the ignition.

He had. Fool. Her heart started to race in her chest.

He was a foot too far away for her to land a good kick, but when he came closer, she was going to be ready.

She needed to disable him and get the hell away. Wherever the road led, it had to be better than being here, waiting for some maniac who did his best work with a hacksaw.

Fueled by determination, she got ready.

But then realized that her chances of escape had got significantly less likely when she saw a white SUV crest a hill, still more than a mile away.

"Finally," Leonard said, relief in his voice.

RAFE FOUND THE quarry easily. The front gate was locked up tight for the night. Over the top of the four-foot gate, he could see several buildings but he decided not to search them. One, because he didn't see a black Cadillac. Two, there were no fresh tracks in the heavy dust. And three, most important, she wasn't here; he could feel it.

He knew that a hunch was about the poorest investigative tool a man could employ, but with Trish, he always had a sense when she was nearby.

He kept driving and turned down the first gravel road. He drove fast, with gravel spraying up behind him. They would lose the light within the hour and that would make the search much more difficult.

He drove with one hand, working the edge of his shirt with the other. He had to find her. He could not lose her now.

His phone rang. It was Chase. "Yeah," Rafe answered.

"You've got me and Bray in my car. My other brother, Cal, is in his own car. Daniel Stone is five minutes behind us."

The cavalry had arrived.

"I've called in air support to assist the Hamerton police in looking for the vehicle," Chase said.

"Thank you." It was a good call but somehow Rafe knew that it wouldn't come in time. "I checked the quarry and am—" he waited a couple of seconds until the sign at the crossroads came into view "—just now crossing Tedrow on Rigger."

Chase said something but it didn't register.

Because at just that moment, when he'd crossed the intersection of the two gravel roads, he'd caught a glimpse of another car crossing Tedrow as well, more than half a mile south.

If the crossroads hadn't been perfectly aligned, he'd never have seen it. He hadn't caught the exact make or model of the vehicle but he knew it was a white SUV going way too fast.

That was enough to make him interested. He interrupted whatever it was that Chase was saying. "I just saw a white SUV going east on the first road south of Rigger. I'm going to try to intercept it."

"We'll be on your six," Chase said, promising backup. "ETA of seven minutes."

Rafe hung up and pushed the speedometer up over a hundred. The next crossroad was farther than he'd anticipated and he cursed the idiots who'd plotted the roads. Finally, he got to it. He slowed to forty-five and made a wide turn. Then he picked up speed from there.

Go. Go. Go. For once his heart and his head were saying the same thing.

DEMÍ MALADUCCI WAS a handsome guy. Didn't look much like a killer, she thought. But when she saw his eyes as he approached, she knew, beyond a shadow of a doubt, that was his intent.

He did not greet Kevin Leonard. He simply extended his arm and Leonard handed him the hacksaw. Demí weighed it in his hand.

"Your husband has caused my family a great deal of trouble," he said.

She licked her lips. "I think he'll be even more focused after this."

Demí laughed. "I have an excellent alibi for tonight. Multiple witnesses who will support that I was nowhere near here. He'll know but he'll never be able to prove it. It will eat him alive."

It would. Rafe loved her. Had always been willing to make great sacrifices to ensure her safety. To know that he failed in the end would be horrible for him.

"Of course, I'll have my own trophy," Demí said.

He reached for her and grabbed her arm. Then he dragged her along, across the scraggly lawn, until he stopped and pushed her down on the ground.

She realized she was next to an open well pit. They were going to put her down there.

"Now I'm going to cut off your hand. And it will give me peace when I look at it later knowing that he knows that you died a slow and painful death, bleeding out, with the rats and the snakes sucking at your blood."

He raised the hacksaw and—

Fell face forward, his body pitching into the well.

Trish rolled away from the pit.

When she looked up, she saw Rafe running across the yard, gun in hand. She realized that he'd shot Demí in the back of the head.

"Hands in the air, Leonard," Rafe yelled.

But he didn't have to shoot him because Kevin Leonard took one look at the man charging toward him, took his own gun, put it in his mouth and pulled the trigger.

Chapter Twenty

Reverend Clara Brown, who had married Trish and Rafe four years ago and most recently performed the marriage services for all three of the Hollister brothers, did the funeral service for Milo. As always, she did a beautiful job. She spoke eloquently about the last years of Milo's life and the relationship he'd had with Summer and Trish.

It was a private service. There was Chase and Raney Hollister, Cal and Nalana Hollister, Bray and Summer Hollister, and Rafe and Trish Wright-Roper, along with just a few of the other employees from the Wright Here, Wright Now Café.

Trish held Summer's hand during the service with Rafe at her other side. He kept an arm around her. He pretty much hadn't stopped touching her since he brought her home last night and made love to her in their bed. It seemed as if he needed the assurance that she was alive and well and truly safe.

They were singing the last song when the back door of the small church opened. A woman, maybe fifty-five, with short, crisp, gray hair, came in.

With a dog.

Duke. With a big, clean bandage wrapped around his middle.

The singing stopped and Trish was running down the aisle.

"I'm sorry," the woman apologized. "I didn't realize there was a service going on."

Trish was on her knees, hugging her sweet dog.

"He wandered up to our house about a week ago. He'd been shot. I've been a nurse for thirty years," she said, "and I thought I could fix him up. I didn't realize he was your dog until I went into town this morning. I drove straight here and the people at the gas station on the main street told me I could find you here."

Trish looked up at her husband, who had tears in his eyes. And then she sat on the dusty floor of the old church and let her big dog climb into her lap.

* * * * *

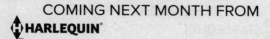
INTRIGUE

Available June 21, 2016

INTRIGUE

Read on for a sneak preview of
AMBUSH AT DRY GULCH
*the conclusion of **BIG "D" DADS: THE DALTONS***
by Joanna Wayne

The last person widowed Carolina Lambert would
consider falling in love with is Jake Dalton. But when
danger forces her to trust the rancher to stay alive, she
realizes only a fool would walk away from a second
chance at happiness…

Carolina Lambert shifted in the porch swing so that she could
look R.J. Dalton, her neighbor, in the eye while they talked. He
rocked back and forth in his chair, sometimes looking at her,
more often staring into space.

Her heart ached at the way his body grew weaker each day.
He had already beaten the odds by more than two years, but
the inoperable tumor in his brain was relentless. It was only a
matter of time, and yet there was a peace to his spirits that she
envied.

He sipped his black coffee, his wrinkled hands so unsteady
that it took both of them to hold his mug. "I reckon Brit told you
that you better get over here and check on the old man while
she took Kimmie in for her checkup."

"No one has to coax me. Spending time with you is always
my pleasure," Carolina said truthfully.

But he was right. Even with a precious baby girl to keep her
busy, his daughter-in-law Brit had pretty much taken over the
job of coordinating the family's schedule so that R.J. was never
alone for more than a few minutes at a time.

"I swear you dropped off St. Peter's coattail, Carolina.

You're the best danged neighbor a scoundrel like me ever had. Best-looking, too. Can't believe you're still running around single. Hugh's been dead, what? Three? Four years now?"

"Four and a half."

"That's a long time to put your life on hold."

"My life's not on hold. I'm busy all the time with my family, friends like you and countless projects."

"Not the same as having a lover."

"Now, what are you doing even thinking about lovers at your age?"

"I'm not dead yet. If I was thirty years younger and not playing hide-and-seek with the grim reaper, I'd be after you quicker than hell can scorch a feather."

"You've done more than your share of chasing women, Reuben Jackson Dalton."

"I caught a few mighty fine ones, too."

"So I've heard."

He smiled, the deep wrinkles around his eyes cutting deep into the almost translucent flesh. "Lived life on my terms, sorry as it was. By rights I ought to be drowning in regrets. If it wasn't for taking your advice about what to do with my ranch, I would be."

"I can't take credit for you turning your life around."

"You don't have to take it, by jiggers. I'm a-givin' it to you. I offered to give you the Dry Gulch Ranch free and clear. You turned me down. Didn't leave me much choice except to try your idea."

"I suggested you leave the Dry Gulch Ranch to your family. That's not a particularly inventive idea."

"Sounded like crazy talk to me. Leave this ranch and what lottery winnings I had left to a bunch of strangers who wouldn't have tipped their hats if I'd passed them on the street."

"Until they got to know you."

Find out what happens in AMBUSH AT DRY GULCH by Joanna Wayne, available July 2016 wherever Harlequin® Intrigue books and ebooks are sold.

Reading Has Its Rewards

Earn **FREE BOOKS!**

Register at **Harlequin My Rewards** and submit your Harlequin purchases from wherever you shop to earn points for free books and other exclusive rewards.

Plus submit your purchases from now till May 30th for a chance to win a $500 Visa Card*.

Visit **HarlequinMyRewards.com** today

Earn **FREE** REWARDS Join Today! HarlequinMyRewards.com

MYR16R1

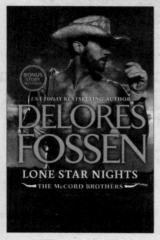

THE WORLD IS BETTER WITH

Romance

Harlequin has everything from contemporary, passionate and heartwarming to suspenseful and inspirational stories.

Whatever your mood, we have a romance just for you!

Connect with us to find your next great read, special offers and more.

f /HarlequinBooks

🐦 @HarlequinBooks

www.HarlequinBlog.com

www.Harlequin.com/Newsletters

⟨H⟩ HARLEQUIN®

A *Romance* FOR EVERY MOOD™

www.Harlequin.com